A FAMILY FOR GOOD

TALL, DARK AND DRIVEN BOOK 6

BARBARA DELEO

FANCY A FREE NOVELLA?

Waiting on Forever—*Alex's story*—*is the prequel to the Tall, Dark and Driven series and is available **exclusively** and **free** for subscribers to Barbara's reader list.*

You can claim your free novella at the end of this book!

1

*N*icosia, Cyprus

Five minutes.

If she could make it through the next five minutes without shattering into tiny pieces and skidding across this shiny marble floor, Liv Bailey could face another day.

She could do five minutes. She'd done it to have blood drawn, or a tooth extracted . . .

In the next five minutes, she'd confront the man she'd once loved. She'd sit down with Markus Panos, discuss the future of the precious newborn twins in his care, and tell him she intended to take them away with her.

Then she'd leave him behind, as fast as she possibly could.

She'd done that before—left, that is—and though two years ago she'd done it to keep her sanity and life intact, the remembered pain of having to leave her heart behind back then stabbed like needles behind her travel weary eyes.

But things were different now.

Now, the past came second to babies she knew she'd love as her own.

She was desperate to see them.

They *had* to make this work. She and Markus owed it to her best friend, Polly, and to the baby girls left motherless when Polly had died so unexpectedly.

Markus could never be anything other than an Indiana Jones in a two-thousand-dollar suit, while she valued the quiet life . . . no risks, no injuries, *no heartache.*

Polly wouldn't rest in peace if she knew her best friend had left her babies with someone who lived life on the edge. She and Polly had known each other since meeting in a foster home at age nine. They'd been like sisters and had promised they'd be godmother to each other's first child.

"He shouldn't be much longer," the woman behind the desk said with a heavy Greek accent, and Liv nodded, absently looking around the walls while her stomach churned.

What *was* this place? With everything written in Greek, she couldn't guess what kind of business he was in. She'd expected the taxi from the airport to take her to an inner-city law firm, not a huge building on the outskirts of Nicosia, the island's largest city.

She could be in any reception area anywhere in the world, except the fittings in this one—the marble floor, the chestnut leather couches—indicated that whatever happened in this company, it was very successful.

"You have a hotel?"

Heat arced through her as she swept her gaze around. And just like that, Markus was there making polite conversation, and the last two years tumbled back in on themselves as she looked into the depths of his rich brown eyes.

She swallowed and stood on liquid legs, willing away the burn of longing she'd known would flame as soon as she saw him. Her heart bruised her chest wall as it hammered ever faster.

Not a muscle on his perfectly tanned face moved; not a blink, not a twitch, not even a hint of emotion or remembrance crossed his sculpted jaw. He stood like one of the ancient statues housed in the museums only a few miles from here—taut and male and with a history she knew as well as her own.

She smoothed down her skirt and, to cover any tremble in her voice, employed her best business tone. "Markus. You *are* here." Not quite the practiced and confident words of reunion she'd dreamed of.

Five minutes.

"I didn't expect you 'til tomorrow," he said as he flicked through papers on the reception desk. "I'm sorry, but as I'm unavailable for the rest of the afternoon, my PA will arrange a more appropriate time for a meeting."

Clutching her folder tighter, she tried to right the tilt everything had suddenly acquired. "We need to talk about Phoebe and Zoë now," she said and threw a quick glance at the receptionist, who'd drawn in a noisy breath. "We need to make plans. I'm grateful for what you've done, but Polly would've wanted *me* to be guardian of the girls. I need to take them back to Brentwood Bay with me. I need to take them home."

Her shoulders slumped.

There. She'd said it in one big rush. It was out in the open, and she held her breath waiting for his response.

Something crossed his face—a softening at the name of her best friend—and Liv could see the composed busi-

3

nessman replaced by the protective partner who'd once melted her heart time and again.

"There won't be any fighting."

His words coiled tight around her, emphasizing the strength and defense in his voice.

She'd heard that tone two years ago. When she'd had to save herself before she fell apart . . .

Markus Panos had taken too many risks. The same sort of risks that cost Liv's biological parents their lives. If you loved someone, if they depended on you, you safeguarded your life. It was as simple as that.

"I see you've come prepared." He looked down at the folder of custody and emigration papers she clutched in her hand.

"We have an appointment with Child and Family Services tomorrow to discuss custody and the girls' long-term care. Can you make it?"

"Of course."

Did he honestly feel no connection to her? Did he not remember what they'd shared? Or had he been too affected by what she'd had to do in the past?

He spoke in Greek to the receptionist, who pursed her magenta lips before stalking past them to an inner office.

Liv sighed and shook her head. "I can't imagine how hard this must've been on you."

"I've done what was necessary. What Polly asked me to do in her final hours."

"I'm sure it's been a struggle." Her voice quavered at the thought of everything that had happened in the last few weeks, but she forced herself to say it all. "Polly dying, the funeral, wondering how to take care of the girls . . . I don't know how you've managed to cope, but I'm ready to take over."

He slowly lifted his gaze to hers, and for the first time, she noticed the pinched skin around his tired eyes.

"You know it's the best thing for everyone, don't you? Phoebe and Zoë . . ." Her throat ached over the words. "They need a mother."

"What they need is security. *Consistency*."

Liv bit her lip. She was so thankful he'd rescued the girls when Polly had no one else to turn to. Liv had done everything she could to track Polly down after she'd stopped replying to Liv's texts, but she'd drawn a blank until Markus had called her with the devastating news.

She spoke more softly. "You shouldn't be expected to look after newborn twins."

A muscle in his jaw flexed twice.

"Where are Phoebe and Zoë now?"

His strong, chiseled face darkened and his thick-lashed brown eyes flashed. "They're safe and well."

"But are they *your* babies? I'm assuming they aren't, since you didn't stop me coming here."

A shudder dropped through her center. The question had slipped out before she could catch it. They hadn't discussed the matter of paternity on the phone. She'd assumed, when he hadn't told her to mind her own business and stay away, that he wasn't their father.

"The babies are my responsibility."

It wasn't a real answer, but she had to go on believing he wasn't their dad. If she didn't push doubts and questions away now, she wouldn't have the strength to see this through.

He leaned a little closer as if to make a connection, but then his lips tightened and the air between them sparked. He dropped his head and looked away.

"You've come from Geneva?" He spoke quietly, ignoring the paternity question hanging in the air.

"Yes, I've been living there, but I'll be returning to Brentwood Bay now, of course."

Brentwood Bay, the place where they'd met and fallen in love so many years ago.

"I trust you've found a hotel for the next few days?"

"Yes, thank you," she said with ridiculous formality. She placed her bag on the countertop to stress the fact she'd be staying here until she got what she'd come to secure. "But I imagine I'll be here longer than a few days. Custody and emigration could take a while."

He stayed silent, the angle of his head indicating he was sizing up her response and not necessarily agreeing with it.

She tried a smile. "The hotel's in the middle of Nicosia, by a lovely old stone wall."

He nodded. "You have everything you need?"

"For now."

He was standing an inch too close . . . and he was too intensely masculine, too rigidly beautiful. He was everything she'd ever wanted in a man, and everything she could never have.

Loving Markus Panos had almost destroyed her once. *Never again.*

Frustrated, she turned away from the power of his stare and noticed something strange, something she'd sensed while she sat waiting. She lifted her chin and inhaled.

Lemon.

The whole place smelled of lemon. Not the antiseptic aroma of a citrus floor cleaner or the sickly synthetic scent of artificial air freshener. This smelled like *real* lemon, the sharp tang of a pitcher of homemade lemonade, or the bite of a cool lemon mousse. Very strange for an office environment—but beautiful.

Returning to meet his proud stare—the one that used to make her feel special, cherished—she cleared her throat and balled her free hand into a private fist, fighting the overwhelming desire to get mad at this intensely uncomfortable situation. She wanted something—two things—very badly, and he was the only one who could give them to her.

"Do you live close?"

Be polite, stay calm.

His words were flat. "There's no need to talk about me." With a self-controlled click, he locked the door she'd closed on him two years ago.

She raised her eyes to the ceiling and counted to three. "Markus, I know you said you were the only person Polly knew in Cyprus, but she would've wanted *me* to have custody of the girls if anything happened to her. She had no relatives, and we were best friends. We shared all the highs and lows in our lives, and we *trusted* each other. So, either we talk now, or it'll have to be done through lawyers."

He blinked slowly, the way she remembered, and her heart skipped a beat as he leaned closer again. And then another short sentence. "I'll give you fifteen minutes."

He turned then and walked down a marbled corridor, and Liv scolded herself for not handling this better. She wished she could just *talk* to him, without feeling she had to prove why she should have custody of the girls.

Striding to keep up with him, she stole quick glances at the huge Grecian artworks on the walls in the sharp light shining down from the atrium ceiling.

When they reached the lift, he swiped a card and stood still, staring straight ahead. She couldn't, wouldn't, allow her hungry eyes a glance as she stood rigid, but she could sense him, smell him—a fragrance of newly hewn wood and cinnamon. The scent of Markus.

He was everything she remembered—mysterious, but with a zest for life that seemed to radiate from every part of him.

A jolt of unbidden awareness ran through her.

She concentrated on the lift too, her heart hollow. He'd always been so animated, dynamic . . . not silent and angry. He'd been a lot like Polly really.

Polly . . .

Tears threatened again, but she shoved them away. Now was the time to be strong.

His office was on the top floor, and Markus held the door open as she walked in.

The panorama beyond almost took her breath away. Stretching out to the stark hills in the distance, it took in high rise buildings and ancient churches in terracotta and beige—the colors of the desert—as well as the boulevards dotted with palm trees, and everything shimmered as the Middle Eastern sun tracked to its high point in the sky.

The smell of lemon was gone, but it was replaced by the rich, buttery scent of nuts. Hazelnuts. Her brow creased as she looked around for the source, but nothing was obvious.

"I'm sorry for your loss." Markus indicated a chair before his desk, and Liv sat, although he stayed standing.

"And yours. The last time we spoke was just after your brother died . . . and now we've lost Polly."

The only time they'd spoken after their breakup was when she'd heard from friends back home that Andoni, Markus's brother, had died. She'd phoned him when he was back in Brentwood Bay for the funeral, and she could tell his heart was breaking all over again. He'd said his focus was on supporting Andoni's twin Alex and his parents, and he'd thanked her for her call.

He rolled his lips together. "Yes, it's been difficult."

So formal. Her heart dropped. No one witnessing this would believe they'd been lovers two years ago.

As she settled into the cushioning comfort of the leather seat, her heartbeat kicked up a gear. The strain of seeing him again was replaced by a desperate need to make a connection with him now. Time for honesty.

"What happened between you and Polly, Markus?" The words rushed out with less subtlety than she'd hoped, and heat lit her cheeks.

His throat moved in an awkward swallow, and he looked down briefly before tilting his head and fixing his gaze on her. "Polly was living in Italy and in trouble. I believe she told you that. She'd been running from some things in her past and contacted me to help. I arranged for her to fly to Cyprus and shortly after the girls' birth she became very ill. I don't think either of us . . ." He stopped, and Liv watched his Adam's apple move up and down in tight jumps.

The honest nature of his words, his real emotion and his attempt to explain were not what she'd expected, and her chest pulled tight. She *so* wanted to believe he wasn't their father . . . that he and Polly hadn't . . .

He clearly didn't want to say more, and what right did she have now to ask him something so intimate? But she had to know. If he was Phoebe and Zoë's father, then no matter how strongly she felt about him having custody, she had no legal rights here.

"I have to know. It changes—"

"Of course you do, and you will. But not right now. After we've met with Child and Family Services, I'll explain everything. But not before."

9

He'd cut across her words with such pace and passion that her mouth remained open as he hurried on. "Phoebe and Zoë are fine. They're being taken care of as they should be."

Although she wanted to press him further, she was pulled up by the way his voice and face softened when he talked about the girls; her heart sped at the way their names fell effortlessly from his mouth. "Who by?" she asked instead.

"They're with a nanny while I'm at work, until I can arrange something more satisfactory."

Uncomfortable at being on this side of the desk—at a decided disadvantage—Liv pulled herself higher in her chair. "When Polly found out she was pregnant, she asked me to be godmother as we'd always agreed. So, unless . . ." Unless he *was* the girls' father.

Wordlessly, he did the slow blink thing again and crossed muscular arms across his taut chest. Her heart thundered and her mouth dried at the thought that he was closed to her.

She pushed on. "She couldn't possibly have imagined things would turn out like this . . ."

"She told you she had escalated blood pressure? That they were worried about her even before the birth?"

A curl of nausea crept its way from her stomach to her throat. No words would come.

"She *told* you her life was in danger?"

Her throat tightened and the smell of nuts became stronger, sickening. All Liv knew was that Polly was pregnant and in Italy with a boyfriend who had a terrible temper. Liv had urged Polly to get away from the guy, suggested she should talk to a lawyer, and then Polly had stopped replying to her texts. Sick with worry, Liv had called all the people they knew in common, rung welfare agencies and the American consulate in Italy, but hadn't found a trace of her. What if she'd tried harder, gotten on a plane sooner and kept hunting until she'd found her beautiful friend? How might things have been different?

"Could I have a glass of water?" She finally managed to force the words out.

He pushed a button at his desk and spoke quickly to someone, the metallic cut of his foreign words making her feel no better. She'd heard his Mom and Dad speak Greek back in Brentwood Bay but never Markus. They'd been lovers. So deeply committed to each other. She'd believed they'd always be together. The reality that he was a stranger now dug painfully deep.

"You knew she was having problems?" His tone was gentler.

The first personal words he'd given her, they brought him—the old Markus—so close she could almost feel him, and her voice quavered as she replied. "Yes. She said her boyfriend had hit her once or twice, but when I tried to discuss it with her, she'd shut down. If only I . . ."

"This must've been a huge shock then." He leaned against the side of the desk, his mouth moving into a soft smile. The door opened and a young woman carried in a silver tray bearing two bottles of mineral water and two squat crystal tumblers. She placed the water and glasses on the desk and left.

He continued. "She said she was planning to let you know she was in Cyprus, but she went into early labor and became very sick. I promised that if anything happened, I'd arrange for Phoebe and Zoë to have the best possible care, and that I'd contact you at the first opportunity . . . which I did."

He unscrewed a bottle and poured the water into a glass before passing it to her. Her hand looked pale and small against his, and for a moment, she remembered how secure she felt when he used to hold it. "It was difficult to track you down," he said.

She heard the insinuation in his voice. The implied question about how stable, how reliable she'd be in the future forced her to reply. "You know the fragrance world," she said, hating that she had to explain. "I travel a lot and was at a conference in Paris when you called. But that'll all change when I take Phoebe and Zoë back to Brentwood Bay. My foster parents want to help me take care of the girls, and when I'm ready I can take on new development work in the US arm of the business."

He walked over to the window and stood with his back to her. The fingers of one hand drummed his other elbow. He'd done that in the past when he'd thought deeply about something.

No, she would *not* remember.

He spoke again; his voice cool, controlled. "This is a difficult situation. I'm custodian of two vulnerable children whose existence I didn't know of ten days ago. I must be certain—"

"The *custodian* . . ." His choice of word caused her throat to catch.

His face read irritation, but his voice remained steady. "As Polly asked, they're under my guardianship and arrangements have been made for their care."

She pushed back her chair as she stood. "I know you've stepped into a terrible situation, and I'm so grateful for it. But you've done everything you need to, and now I'm here to take over. Polly was in state care as a child, so the girls have no grandparents or aunts and uncles. The babies are fragile and ... motherless, Markus."

She sucked in her top lip, grateful he was still turned away so he couldn't see it wobble. The grief she'd kept bottled up for the past few weeks, as she'd tried to establish Polly's whereabouts, was now inching its way out.

"I'm sorry." She swayed, her legs barely able to hold her. "This is a very emotional time and I want..." Her words were a tight whisper. "I just want what Polly would've wanted."

He lifted his square jaw higher so the shadow on it appeared a shade darker. "I completely understand that, but you must see the position I'm in. Polly asked me to do my absolute best for her daughters, and I intend to do just that."

His words thudded in her ears, and she fell back a step as if she'd been struck.

"You don't think being with me would be the best option? Are you referring to what happened with us?"

"Of course, I am, Olivia. You walked out on our relationship without any warning, and aside from that, you've never lived in one place any real length of time. The girls need consistency now. Stability."

It was the first time he'd said her name, and the way his voice caressed and smoothed the syllables, as he'd done so many times before, softened her response to his suggestion. "I'm here for Phoebe and Zoë now, aren't I?"

He shrugged. "Anyone can turn up for a day."

She swallowed. Was she alienating him with her words? But she knew deep in her heart they had to work together. They had to acknowledge the power of the past—their intimate knowledge of each other— and then bulldoze those great boulders out of their way.

It was time to change focus. "I really want to see them, Markus." She couldn't cover the crack in her voice.

He rubbed a hand across his jaw, and she let out a slow breath. "I know you're protecting them, and that's what I knew you'd do. We've got a lot to go through before all the paperwork's done, but I have to see them. See the last two things Polly touched." The tears fought their way to the surface, and she struggled to keep them at bay. "This is unexpected for me as well." Her voice tripped as a tear began its path down her cheek. "At least let me see them. Please."

He began to speak. "It's—" Then his gaze met hers and the look on his face changed.

Could he still care, at least enough to be moved by her sadness? She dragged the inside of her wrist across her cheek. Despite wanting to give in to the weight of her grief, she *had* to stay in control. For Phoebe and Zoë.

"Of course, you can see them." He looked at his watch. "At five o'clock this afternoon. They fed at seven this morning, so if their routine's on track, that should work." He moved briskly across the room to the door, clearly expecting her to leave.

"Where? Where should I meet you?" Anticipation fluttered in her stomach.

"There's a square, right in front of the Byzantine Museum. We'll be there at five o'clock."

"I could come to your home," she said suddenly. "So the girls aren't unsettled."

His features moved again, and the curtain of his defenses closed once more. "The square is fine. I must protect Phoebe and Zoë in the meantime, Olivia, from anything that might compromise their stability. For now, they're with me, and until I get an indication that you have their best interests at heart, that you're not going to run when everything gets too difficult . . ." He nodded. "That's the way it'll remain."

Despite being late afternoon, the majestic Cypriot sun sent a blanket of heat across the ancient square. In the distance, people sat around tables, talking and drinking long coffees, and a priest, like a blackbird on the wing, made his way up the steps of a church.

Although she'd traveled all over the world for business, it was rare for Liv to be somewhere foreign on her own. Normally she'd have drivers and personal assistants to take care of things for her, but she'd chosen to take this on alone. Alone with the man she'd once loved and with her sense of inadequacy at the possibility of being a parent . . .

But she'd steeled herself, and here she was.

Phoebe and Zoë were all that mattered in the world, and she was desperate to see them.

The smell of barbecued food teased her senses, and her stomach growled. She hadn't eaten since breakfast. In fact, she'd eaten very little in the last few days since learning of her best friend's death.

Markus had called a week ago. He'd been polite, detached on the phone at first, but gentle when he gave her the heart-breaking news. Much of what he'd said had been lost between Liv's sobs, but she'd gained enough understanding to know she had to get to the girls as quickly as she could.

She scanned the square, wringing her hands at the thought of seeing Markus again. A sense of awareness flushed her cheeks as she turned, and then her heart hit her throat.

There he was. There *they* were. Markus and the girls were turned slightly away from her at the edge of the square.

For some reason, she'd expected a nanny, or his mother, would be with him to take responsibility for the tiny babies —that he'd have very little to do with their day-to-day care.

But Markus, dressed in a sleek black suit, and looking more protective, more natural than she could ever have imagined, stood alone, carefully rocking a double stroller backward and forward.

Phoebe and Zoë—all that was left of Polly—were just a few feet from Liv now, and she instinctively moved forward, her breath jamming her already clogged chest.

One of the babies let out a cry and Markus bent down, carefully removed the sunshade, and lifted a tiny bundle into his arms.

And the power of seeing it—the love and wonder and longing that swept the length of her body and gripped tight around her heart—made Liv falter.

She'd assumed he'd be the same hurried and hyper man she remembered. That he'd want her to take the babies off his hands as quickly as possible so he could get on with taking risks and putting himself first.

But the way he held that precious gift of a girl in the crook of his arm, with his head bent toward her face and his lips moving in a whisper, made something unravel in Liv's chest. In her wildest dreams, she'd never have believed Markus Panos could be so giving, so responsible.

She made her way slowly toward them. As she got nearer, she couldn't speak, the muscles of her throat too crushed by the beauty of what she saw: father and . . . daughter?

As he returned the quietened baby to the stroller, she

edged closer and could now see Phoebe and Zoë as two perfect bundles. Their identical heads, as round and smooth as river stones, peeked above dusky pink blankets, and their tiny hands were placed in the same position by each of their rosebud mouths.

Fresh tears filled her eyes as she knelt and held out a hand to touch. The warmth of two little bodies seeped into her soul. Their breath, like a forgotten whisper, reached her straining ears.

She sensed Markus step away.

The sadness of the whole situation scrambled her thoughts. Why had Polly been so secretive in her life recently? Why had she never even mentioned meeting up with Markus? And why, oh why, hadn't Liv found her friend in time?

Despite witnessing Markus's care with the girls just now, he'd said he saw himself as *custodian* to these precious babies. Treating their happiness as a problem to solve or a challenge to tackle wasn't enough. They needed a loving parent.

Not being a relative to Polly meant Liv's legal rights were zero, but although her experience with children was nil, she knew to her deepest heart that she *would* love these children as madly and deeply as if they were her own.

"They're gorgeous," she whispered, hoping she could make a deeper connection with Markus, lay the groundwork for the discussion that had to be continued. "I never imagined they'd be so tiny."

He stood by, silently watching, and Liv rose from where she knelt to create some link between them, between him and her need to reach out, to smile, to connect . . . "I'm sorry you've had to become involved with this. If I'd . . . If things had worked out differently, I could've been here and . . ."

Sorrow crashed over her. "I couldn't find her. I didn't even know she'd left Italy. But none of that matters now. What's important is that I'm here to take the girls back to Brentwood Bay as Polly would've wanted."

She should've done more, and the pain of knowing she'd let Polly down seared deep.

He removed his glasses in the slow, deliberate way that reminded her how strong and confident he was.

"We'll work this out, Olivia. For the sake of Phoebe and Zoë, we'll find the best possible future for them, but for their stability in the meantime, it's best they stay with me."

He spoke as if she were a stranger, not a woman he'd once held and said he'd rather stop living than be without her. Her heart spasmed as she forced herself to speak, and frustration muscled its way between sorrow for all she'd lost and the measured tone of her words.

She breathed long and deep. "What you're doing, what you've done for Polly and the girls, is amazing, Markus, and I know it'll take some time to work things out."

He gripped the handle of the stroller before he spoke with quiet conviction, his words wrapping her tight. "I've only done what someone committed to the best for Phoebe and Zoë would do, and I hope you've got that sort of commitment too."

Bam.

In one sentence he'd reached the heart of this entire dilemma, past and present together, and she ached. Because she'd left him in the past, he didn't think she had the commitment to be there for the girls for the rest of their lives.

She pushed the past aside—she couldn't let it matter now. All that mattered was Phoebe and Zoë, and she wasn't going to leave here without them.

2

*L*iv sat in the waiting room of the court appointed social worker the next morning, numbly staring at a poster.

Aphrodite's Rock, it announced. A collection of rocks that stuck out from a cobalt sea, with one in particular rising majestically above the others as waves crashed around it. Underneath was written: *The birthplace of the goddess. The island of love. Cyprus.*

Here she was—on this island of love—and the man who'd once meant more to her than any other was outside on the pavement talking into his phone, instead of inside sitting beside her.

The irony caused breath to rush from her lips as she thought about what had brought her to this island. This might be the place Aphrodite was born, but the goddess of love wasn't doing her any favors right now.

She ached to see Phoebe and Zoë again, to breathe in their soft baby scent and feel their tiny fingers curl tight around hers.

"Ms. Bailey," a woman said as she stepped out from the

interior office. "I'll see you now." Although she looked Cypriot, with her black hair pulled into a pony tail, she spoke perfect English, with a Canadian accent.

Liv turned and hesitated, the fingers of one hand kneading her palm as she waited to catch Markus's eye through the window. He looked so distant, so obviously interested in things that didn't concern her anymore, and part of a life she'd never know.

He turned and saw her, his chin kicking up in acknowledgment, and so Liv pulled her shoulders back and walked past the social worker, every muscle taut in anticipation of the custody discussion they'd be having this morning.

"Now, we can begin," the woman said from behind her desk once they were all seated. Markus sat on Liv's left. His proximity—and trademark wood and cinnamon scent—soothed her stretched nerves.

"I'm Ana-Maria Clerides, the social worker in this case. I assume everyone's comfortable if this interview is conducted in English?"

They both nodded.

"We're here today because Ms. Bailey has filed an application to take the children in question to the United States," Ana-Maria said.

Liv nodded and was aware of Markus, motionless at her side. How would he react today? Would he agree, protest, or do something different altogether? She hadn't seen him since yesterday in the square and wished she had some idea whether her presence had softened or strengthened his resolve.

She let her breath go slowly as the silence lengthened and he said nothing.

He was still holding back, still not giving in as easily as she'd hoped, but then he wouldn't be the deep-thinking, caring man she'd known if he'd immediately given up the girls and walked away. For a moment she let that memory of him sit softly in her chest.

"These babies were born in Cyprus, Ms. Bailey. So, it's up to the local authorities to make decisions about their welfare." Ana-Maria nodded toward Liv before moving her gaze to Markus. "And, as the names of neither the babies' father nor their next of kin were put on hospital records, and Mr. Panos was listed as a local contact, he's been granted temporary custody."

The social worker sat back in her chair and regarded them both, her brow tightening. "And now you wish for them to be taken to the US?"

"Yes," Liv replied immediately, hoping Markus maintained his silence. "I've explained everything in my application."

He crossed his ankles and opened his mouth but before he could reply, the social worker continued.

"We do, of course, put the children first in these sorts of situations," she said. "It's not just a matter of who puts forward the best case for custody. I'm sure you can appreciate that we have to be certain Phoebe and Zoë will receive the highest level of care now that their mother has died. In most situations, we'd expect the other parent—the father, in this case—to have physical custody."

Parents. The word settled itself deep inside Liv, touching a part she'd kept carefully locked down for two whole years. The thought of being completely responsible for a tiny human had always terrified her and reminded her of her own devastation when she'd lost her mother and father in a skydiving accident. And because she'd always pushed away discussion of it when she and Markus were together, being here now, fighting him for that right, was causing her more pain than she'd imagined.

The social worker's words cut through her thoughts. "Since your temporary custody order was granted, Mr. Panos, the authorities at the hospital have raised some queries about the long-term placement of the girls," Ana-Maria said. "Apparently you weren't at the babies' birth. Is that right?"

"That's correct."

"You realize that regardless of whether you or Ms. Bailey is granted final custody, the court has a duty of care to establish paternity. We wouldn't want someone shirking their child support responsibilities regardless of whether these babies stay here or go to the United States."

Her insinuation was clear. They wanted Markus to take a paternity test.

"Of course," he said coolly, and Liv breathed a private sigh of relief. Although she wasn't sure why he'd said he couldn't tell her the truth until after this meeting, at least now she'd find out one way or the other.

Ana-Maria continued. "If, after a DNA test, Mr. Panos is found not to be the father, there will be quite a process to go through before final custody is determined. We will also need to investigate whether there are any grandparents who might have a custody claim. If we find no immediate family, the family court judge will decide who's the most suitable guardian on the basis of psychological and social assessments, as well as visits with each of you and the girls. Of course, the best result in that case would be if you could come to a custody agreement yourselves and then have it ratified by the court."

Liv sat forward, the thought that this was going to take longer than she'd anticipated causing an ache in her temple.

"That sounds complicated. Polly had no biological family, so how long until the girls could leave with me?" she asked, trying to keep her words steady.

Ana-Maria's voice was gentle. "Assuming your custody application was successful, approximately a month or two."

"And, in the meantime, what will happen to Phoebe and Zoë? Do they remain with Markus or come to me?"

"As I said, the social worker at the hospital has some concerns about the unusual nature of this case and doesn't want the children in an unsettled environment. If there's a significant dispute about custody, we could place them with a foster family."

"No!"

They'd spoken as one, with Markus's response as forceful as Liv's desperate one, and she turned in shock to look at him.

Sparks flew from his chestnut irises—eyes Liv had fallen into a million times, eyes that knew her.

She couldn't bear to think of someone else looking after Phoebe and Zoë. If there'd been someone who'd fought for her as a child, she'd never have ended up on her own. She'd been exceptionally lucky and had two wonderful years with one foster family when she was fourteen, but then their circumstances had changed and she'd had to go back into state care. Polly had never found a real home either. These babies were so little and defenseless, and they needed to be with people who loved them now.

"You have another solution?" Ana-Maria's soft gaze swung from Liv to Markus and back again. "Something to guarantee their stability?"

"They can live with me, and Markus could visit whenever he wanted," Liv said immediately. "I'll have them until this is sorted out. We'll make it work."

She leaned forward again, willing Ana-Maria to say she could have Phoebe and Zoë for the next four weeks.

"With respect, Ms. Bailey, you're not a blood relation, nor a Cypriot citizen, and a hotel room will not provide the sort of environment the babies require."

"They can stay with me," Markus said. "I've had them since they were born. They have everything they need where they are, I know their routine, and Olivia would always be welcome in my home."

His last words caused a hum in Liv's chest, and trying to ignore it, she swung her gaze to Ana-Maria to wait for her decision.

The social worker drummed a pencil on her desk as she looked first at Liv, then Markus. "I can see you both feel strongly about this situation. I'll leave you alone for five minutes, in which time I'd like you to come up with a plan for how custody and visitation would work in the interim, otherwise . . . Well, you know the alternative."

When the door clicked shut behind her, Markus stood, pulled his suit jacket off and placed it over the back of his chair, before shrugging his shoulders. "They can't go to strangers," he said, avoiding her eyes which still smoldered from their connection minutes ago. "We can't let that happen. I've begun bonding with them and you—" He trailed off, but the determined look was back.

Not only was he intent on protecting Phoebe and Zoë until he knew they were safe, but he was concerned about bonding as well.

Liv hadn't considered bonding.

Maybe they could agree on something, work together and be a family for the time it took to determine custody.

"We must make it work," he said as he dug a strong hand through his shiny black waves. "You're in a hotel. No place for newborn twins. They need warmth, fresh air . . . stability." His look was loaded with innuendo.

"I could hire a house for a month, set it up as I would at home," she said. "I wouldn't be working if I was with them for the next few weeks, and they'd spend their whole time with me." Her heart thumped.

He shook his head. "But it wouldn't be fair to the girls, transporting them backward and forward. They'd be unsettled."

She stopped talking. Her suggestions were futile. It was no use. Of course, Phoebe and Zoë should stay with him for now.

"You're welcome to visit any time," he said quietly, looking at her with such intensity it knocked her emotionally backward. "You could spend whole days at my home if you'd like."

She swallowed as every reason why that was a terrible idea raced through her brain. In the same house with the man whose touch she'd once loved—the same touch she'd ached for and dreamed of the last two years? The man who'd been everything to her before she'd realized a future with him—with his children—would be impossible?

"I'll take the girls to my beach house at Aphrodite's Rock," he continued. "There's more room, so I can work from home at night, and we could care for Phoebe and Zoë during the day. Together."

For a minute, the beauty of that image settled in her mind before, with heart-crunching sadness, the truth struck her. He wanted to watch her with the girls, ensure she was capable of being the parent she'd told him she could be, before he'd give them up.

He didn't trust her. Didn't trust she'd make a commitment and stick with it. And that simple knowledge killed something deep inside.

He spoke with precision, shattering her comforting dreams with his practical reality. "Bottom line? We both want what's best for Phoebe and Zoë. Agreed?"

She nodded. Her throat was so thick the words wouldn't come, but he was right. The babies, it was all about the babies now, not Liv and Markus.

"The best thing for them is to be in one place surrounded by people who care about them and see their needs as paramount."

She blinked. "Right."

If only she could resist the urge to look at him, could turn away, could feel—or at least pretend—indifference. He wanted to watch her, but only to know if she was finally capable of settling down and giving in to love.

He was right to still want to keep Phoebe and Zoë protected, and even if the physical closeness to him destroyed her emotionally, it would mean she could really bond with the girls in the eyes of the court and show she was the right parent for them.

His eyes shone with nothing but reason and logic. None of the desire from the past, none of the fire that had burned when they were together.

A knock at the door and the social worker came back in. She carried a handful of papers and wore an expression that indicated she meant business.

"I have the documentation here to put the girls into foster care, and I also have papers you could sign for a temporary custody and visitation agreement. Can I remind you that however you decide to arrange things, the court will frown on any indication of disharmony between the two of you." She sat down and raised her pen. "So, Ms. Bailey, Mr. Panos—what's your decision?"

Markus leaned an arm on the southern wall of his cliff-top beach house and looked out through the massive picture window across to Aphrodite's Rock and the ever-changing Mediterranean Sea surrounding it.

A storm was brewing, and black thunderheads were rolling in from the south. Occasionally, a shaft of brilliant sunshine would illuminate a spot on the sea's surface and turn it golden before disappearing again just as quickly.

The rapidly changing seascape mirrored his change of heart. Liv was about to appear for her first visit at his house, and he didn't know if he was prepared.

To have her back within touching distance . . . Something he hadn't imagined in his wildest dreams, something he'd never expected he'd have to deal with.

When he'd seen her in his office four days ago, he'd employed every trick known to man to stop the fire that sparked and gained heat through his body. He'd succeeded well enough then, but how would it feel dampening down that reaction day after day?

A car pulled into the driveway, and he turned away from the window, disgusted by his own eagerness for any sight of her.

He couldn't deny her claim to the babies, or her desire to take them back to the States, as Polly had no relatives. When she knew the truth about their paternity, she'd see her goal as unobstructed.

But he hadn't counted on how he'd feel about Phoebe

and Zoë—the swell in his chest every time he looked at them, cared for them, watched them change from day to day. At least for now, he was the parent in every way that counted, and before he agreed to Liv's claim, he had to be sure . . .

He sat with a thump on the sleek leather couch and waited for her entrance. He heard Petro, his housekeeper, open the front door and welcome her, but he stayed exactly where he was, even picking up a thick supply contract to keep his gaze from drifting to the foyer.

"Hello, Markus."

He stayed focused on the papers, reading the same sentence over and over. "I'll be with you in a moment." He wanted a minute to prepare himself, to make sure seeing her didn't jolt him the way it had a few days ago.

The silence of the house was punctuated by the soft shush of her dress against the couch and the high whistle of wind outside. "The girls haven't arrived yet," he managed to say through a concrete jaw.

And when she didn't answer, he looked up slowly.

She was a vision in red. From the soft ballet-type shoes to the floaty skirt, his gaze fed on her slim brown legs up to—

He froze.

She held a suitcase.

"You said you had plenty of room," she said quickly. "And as you'll be working from home, I figured that, to save you from complete exhaustion, I may as well make myself useful and help you during the day and night."

The night.

The thought of him meeting Liv in a darkened corridor, when she was warm and mussed from sleep, assaulted his senses.

She placed the suitcase on the floor and sat in the seat

opposite him. "But I need to know for sure before we go any further with this. Are the girls yours, Markus?" She rushed on, before he could answer. "I know it'll come out when paternity tests are done, but I need to hear it from you. Especially now. Are you Phoebe and Zoë's father?"

He crossed his arms and leaned back in his chair. He should've told her the truth earlier and removed the doubts and questions he could see when she'd watched him with the girls. In hanging on to the truth, he'd been protecting Phoebe and Zoë from the Liv he'd known in the past. But what right did he have to keep it from her if she'd changed as much as she said she had? She deserved the truth.

"Polly and I were never in a relationship. I'm not Phoebe and Zoë's father."

Closing her eyes, she breathed deep, and he was stunned by the power of her relief as her shoulders rose then fell. In seconds, he was standing beside her chair.

"You can't say anything to anyone," he said, desperate for her to understand the gravity of this.

"What do you mean?" Her relief was audible in her voice as she trained her gaze on his face.

He spoke quickly, dragging a hand through his hair. "As you know, Polly was in a relationship with a guy in Italy who was violent. When she finally said she'd report him to the police, he threatened her life and the lives of the girls, so she called me to ask for some legal advice. When I knew she was heavily pregnant and possibly in danger I arranged to fly her here so she'd be safe from any threat. She went into labor two days later."

Liv pinched the bridge of her nose as if to stem the fresh sorrow he knew would be raging through her. "I should've been here," she whispered. "I wish she'd told me she was in so much trouble." She curled and uncurled her fingers. "Go on," she said, the words forced out.

"I arranged for private medical care and it was then the doctors realized her blood pressure was dangerously high. She asked me to arrange for the girls' care in the event that anything went wrong."

Liv stared at the floor—her brow furrowed, face ashen— as if trying to make sense of it all before she slowly looked up. "But Ana-Maria, the social worker. You didn't even tell her. When we were in her office, she seemed to think things were strange, but you never told her the truth."

"I can't tell the truth. Not yet, anyway. Everything will be out in the open when the paternity results are done, and hopefully by that time, we can be sure that drunken creep is long gone."

"You did all that for Polly?" she whispered.

Something in his chest pulled as he took the chair beside her, his hand so close he could've touched her if he'd dared. "Of course, I did. And now I've made the commitment, you must see why I need to ensure they're safe, that all their needs will be met? Always?"

She turned to face him. "Of course, I can, Markus, and you need to know that I want exactly the same thing. When you talked about bonding yesterday, it got me thinking. No matter which of us the girls are with long term, the sooner they bond with that person, the better. You said yourself the best thing for Phoebe and Zoë is to be in one place surrounded by people who care about them." Her rigid, unbending gaze held his. "That's why I'm here."

She stopped speaking and her gaze grew wary, as if expecting him to argue, to tell her no, that this wouldn't be happening. Instead, what she said about staying here was logical, reasonable even. What he struggled to believe was that it had come from her.

"I want to see and understand every part of their day, their routine," she continued. "And it wouldn't be fair for me to have the good bits during the day and leave you the tough time at night."

Surely those words weren't spoken by the same woman who'd walked out on him, who'd just up and left when everything got too much for her? *That* Liv hadn't had the capacity to stay and work things through when the going got tough.

This woman was determined.

The thought that she might've changed in the past two years began to unfurl, and a familiar desire took hold of his insides and pulled long and low through his core.

"And what if it doesn't suit me, you staying here?" He was testing her, wanting to hear again that this time she was prepared to fight for something in her life. "What makes you think I haven't got a wife who might object to another woman taking over her house?"

For just a second, her jaw slackened and her eyes grew round, but then she sat straighter. "Then I guess that would mean one of us could get some sleep while the others were feeding the girls."

He couldn't help the smile that tugged at the corner of his mouth at the lengths she'd go to convince him on this. This newfound passion for commitment was unsettling and . . . disturbingly attractive. "Let's get through a day together before we go making any rash decisions."

She sat forward, took her sunglasses from their perch on the top of her head and absently began opening and shutting one of the arms. "But whatever happens, we have to talk about a few things before our full attention is turned to the babies. You said they weren't here yet?"

She hadn't asked whether he did, in fact, have a wife. Did that mean she'd be unmoved if he did? Would she still be determined to carry this through? "My assistant, Eleni, is bringing the girls from my home in Nicosia. I wanted to have everything ready for them before they arrived. And I'd guessed you'd want to talk about the way this would work."

An ever-increasing smile lit her face. "I'm still that predictable?" Her gaze finally met his, and her eyes sparked before she looked past him and stood. "This is quite some beach house." She crossed to the window, still holding her sunglasses in her hand but now tapping them against her thigh. "What a beautiful view, although the weather's made a rapid change. It was sunny when I left the hotel."

"You're looking at Aphrodite's Rock." He made himself stay put, needing to keep physical distance between them. "Legend says that Aphrodite was born out of the sea's foam surrounding the rock."

He deliberately didn't tell her the rest.

She raised a hand above her eyes, as if looking for any evidence a goddess might've walked this way. "That's why Cyprus is known as the island of love."

As soon as she'd said the words, he wanted to back out of the intimacy of this conversation. "It's just a legend," he said quickly, trying to resurrect his guard that had unexpectedly slipped. "Nothing more than a fairy tale."

She swung around then and fixed him with one of her trademark looks of brutal honesty. "Can we really make this work for four weeks, Markus?"

Her eyebrows rose in challenge, and he remembered the little arguments they'd had in the past, about nothing more important than which park to spend the afternoon in.

They'd always ended the same way, those little arguments, with a million kisses and the promise of everlasting love.

She crossed her arms under her breasts and continued to stare.

He'd show her he was committed to seeing this through. He also had a plan to determine whether she'd changed, whether she had the capacity to commit herself to the girls as she claimed. But before he tested it, he wanted to hear a little more about how she imagined this would all work. "It will work if we both want it enough."

"Markus, we can't live under the shadow of resentment for a month. We have to put our past behind us and focus on Phoebe and Zoë."

She'd always been so honest, far too sure of everything in the world. It was her absolute black and white approach to life that had destroyed them before.

He stood and moved toward her, breaking the pact he'd made earlier with himself about distance. "This isn't about us, Liv. It's about the welfare of Phoebe and Zoë. And until we can guarantee their safety and a stable future, their care is the most important thing."

Olivia, he'd meant to keep calling her Olivia. Perhaps she hadn't noticed.

"We can't keep our heads in the sand, Markus. I agree that the girls' welfare is the most important thing, but we owe it to them to be honest with each other. If we're going to get along in the next four weeks and provide the sort of positive atmosphere we want for the babies, we need to be open."

He should've known she'd want to do this—clear the air, be practical and straightforward.

The crunch of tires on the shell driveway outside indicated Eleni had arrived with the babies.

He wanted to say one more thing to her while they were still alone, so he took a step closer. Her eyes widened, rounded a little and the pull of her indicated he was only inches from a touch.

Strangely, he wanted her to really see him this time, to acknowledge who and what he was and that he should've, could've, been the one for her all those years ago.

He risked another step and was so close her heat warmed him. A light, heady and floral scent, probably one of her own creations, surrounded her. Her violet eyes softened, and the last two years disintegrated.

The sound of Eleni climbing the stairs to the door brought him to his senses. He spoke quietly, but with the conviction she'd expect from him. "We will make this work, Olivia. For the sake of Phoebe and Zoë. We will."

And as he watched Liv move quickly to the door, he hoped that, in making it work, he could ignore the siren call of her lips and guard the barrier he'd so carefully built around his heart.

3

$\mathcal{T}$hey were alone —Liv, Markus, and two tiny bundles in baby seats—in this cliff-top mansion, and nobody made a sound.

Slowly, Liv knelt and laid a tentative hand on the petal pink blanket that covered one of the girls. The baby's big brown eyes opened and closed in slow, languid blinks. "Hello, baby girl," she whispered, her voice catching as she stroked the soft cotton covering, and her hand warmed by the tiny body beneath. Every nerve ending hummed with this connection and sang with the love she felt for this tiny child.

She swung her gaze to Markus, her mind gripped by a terrible thought. "Which is which?" she asked, as cold tentacles wrapping around her heart tightened her words. "They're dressed exactly the same! What if we get them mixed up - can you tell who's who?"

Markus was leaning against a dark leather couch watching her, with his head tilted as if in deep thought. The corner of his mouth lifted in the teasing, knowing way that had always sent a spiral of want through her. He had a way of waiting a few moments before replying, almost as if he could communicate without speaking. Even now, it felt like an intimate bond and her pulse quickened. "Not right now, I can't." The warmth of his voice settled on her like a familiar touch. A lover's touch—and she ached for the loss of it.

"Well, we have to find out." She hastily looked away as she got to her feet. "They should be dressed in different clothes or have different bootees or something. We can't go around mixing them up."

Markus crouched by a baby seat, as she'd just done, and laid his broad tan hand across the blanket. Something kicked sharply inside her—a feeling of loss, of desperate want and hope—and for a second she couldn't hear what he was saying.

". . . in the bath. You won't be able to tell the difference then."

Reality dragged her back to what he was saying as he unwrapped the end of one of the blankets to reveal a tiny bootee-clad foot.

So carefully, as if touching a fragile piece of china or removing a delicate butterfly from a cobweb, he took the bootee off and laid it on the floor. "This is Phoebe."

And then Liv saw it. A speck of bright pink nail polish on one of the baby's toenails. She let out a laugh of relief and a shroud of tension lifted from her shoulders.

"I borrowed some nail polish from Eleni and painted one of Phoebe's toenails pink and one of Zoë's red. Chances are the colors will stay on for a while, but even if one wears off, we can tell who the other is. I suppose you'll have some polish so we can maintain it." He gave her a look she couldn't interpret. "You always did like your nail polish, so I thought . . ." He trailed off, but the ghost of a smile lingered.

Her breath caught at the sight of it. He'd liked to tease

her about her femininity, her love of clothes and makeup. He'd been deeply fascinated by her parfumier study, though, so there was always respect behind his words.

"I think I've brought a bottle or five." She let a grin tug at her lips, too. She was still mesmerized by the little foot in his beautiful, strong hand and his thumb stroking a tiny toe.

Although he wasn't the girls' father, the way his eyes softened when he looked at them, and an unspoken emotion that rippled below the surface of his tanned face, indicated he loved them as much as any new dad.

She knelt down to one of three enormous baby bags Eleni had brought and began rummaging. How on earth could two immobile things require so much equipment? Diapers, clothes, boxes of baby wipes and plastic mats— surely they wouldn't need all this?

"What are you looking for?" Markus asked as he carefully replaced the bootee.

"Hats. Different colored hats so we can tell who's who in the meantime. We can dress them in different clothes later, but I'd like to . . ." She held two miniature hats aloft, one lemon and one pink. "Got them. Pink for Phoebe and yellow for Zoë."

He held a hand out, and she passed them to him without looking up, pretending to search for something else in the bag. But the touch of his hand as their skin brushed, just for a second, sent a tingling warmth up her arm.

They were speaking normally to each other, as if the events of two years ago had never happened, as if he hadn't scared the life from her and she hadn't had to leave him.

"They're so quiet," he said, as she carried the bag to the table and started removing stuff and making little piles. "As if they know they've lost their mommy."

Her heart staggered. When she caught his eye as he

looked up from tucking Phoebe's blanket back in, his face was filled with emotion. The same sort of sorrow that kicked her deep in the chest every time she thought of these gorgeous girls without a mother.

A lump hurt her throat as she thought of a life without Polly's spontaneous sunshine and laughter, without even the troubles she'd tumbled into. How would she get through the rest of her life without her oldest friend?

"Right," she said, trying to deflect the unintended connection between them and the hole of emotion she'd fall down if she let herself. "I guess we should get these little ones fed, then down for a sleep."

"Yep." He stood and waited, watching her with the concentrated gaze that had the power to make her knees weak.

If I let it.

"Don't look at me," she said. "I wouldn't know where to start!"

He put both hands low on his hips, causing his black T-shirt to pull taut across his upper arms. "There are tins of formula and baby bottles in one of the bags. I'll do it while you watch the girls."

"No, it's fine," she said. "I want to learn what to do." Again, she'd assumed he'd have Eleni or the nanny do this. That he'd pay someone to make it all easy for him. The fact he hadn't was surprising, and confusing.

"I asked Eleni to find some baby-care books for you in English." He moved to a pile of paperbacks on a side table and flicked through one. "Trouble is, you can read about feeding and routine and how to get a baby to sleep in one of these, but it's always about a single baby. They don't tell you what to do when one baby sleeps all night and the other sleeps all day, or how to cope when one's waking every hour. Maybe we can look online for solutions.

Liv took an unsteady breath. The enormity of what he'd coped with in the last ten days became stinging reality, but knowing that he'd thought about what she'd need to know and organized the books made her heart lighter.

Who was he now? And if he had the capacity for this sort of caring, this sort of unrequited devotion, then why hadn't she seen the depth of it before?

"I'll make a bottle." She struggled to keep her voice calm as one of the girls began to whimper. "Could you pick up Phoebe . . . or is that Zoë . . . while I try and sort this out?"

The whimper became a full-fledged cry, and a cold clutch of panic took hold. "I think she's hungry," she said, pulling more paraphernalia out of bags. "Quick, pick her up before she starts the other one off."

"It's okay, Liv." Markus's voice was warm and calming as the second baby, picking up on her sister's distress, started the same wail. "Do you want me to do it?"

"Bottles!" Liv beamed, despite the rising cries. "And little measures of formula! It's okay," she called over the din. "I've got it. Just hang on!"

Without waiting to see his reaction, she poured the formula into each bottle, put the lids on and shook them. Fine drops of milk flew everywhere—over the marble floor, her silk dress. Oh yeah, bottle teats had holes in them . . .

And warm. Wasn't baby milk supposed to be warm? One of her foster sister's, Claudia, used to test a few drops on the inside of her wrist before she'd feed her baby.

The wailing was a full blast in stereo, and as she picked up the formula tin to work out how to heat the bottle, Markus unclipped the girls from their baby seats.

Greek. The instructions were in Greek! She threw a look

at Markus as he lifted first one baby and then the other into his strong arms.

"I've got the bottles and formula," she said breathlessly. "What do I do now?"

"Put hot water in that container by the sink." He nodded toward the kitchen counter as the girls' cries began to lessen while he held them close. "And put the bottles in to warm up."

She rushed to the sink, and when she looked up, Markus had his back to her, his T-shirt riding up to reveal a strip of deeply tanned skin at his waist. She dragged her gaze to the babies who were now quiet, one perfect head on each of his broad shoulders. Her eyes smarted at the perfection of the scene, the way his strong arms curved around their tiny bodies.

Ten minutes later, Liv sat on the couch opposite Markus, each of them with a feeding baby in their arms. Rain fell heavily against the picture window and the sea in the distance churned wildly.

Markus's head was bent as he watched Phoebe, with his hand absently patting the small pink bundle. Seeing the simple beauty of it, memories of the man she'd fallen in love with long ago jostled their way into her mind. She held a breath as the old feelings touched her.

Remember.

She had to remember his inconsistency, his unreliability, all the reasons she'd left him. But it was so hard when he was being so constant and reliable now. He was so much more in control than she'd expected, so able to cope with the situation he'd been thrown into.

He doesn't really need me here at all.

The unexpected thought stung, and she held Zoë closer.

Having seen, even in the short time she'd been here how

much Markus obviously cared for the babies made her question what had gone wrong between the two of them. What would the four weeks she'd be here do to her?

She'd suggested she could feed the girls herself while he got some work done. But he'd insisted he'd help and hadn't spoken to her since. He wasn't about to let her completely take over the care of the girls. He'd made that quite clear. And if she were truly honest, especially after the circus that feeding them just now had been, she had an awful lot to learn about how to take care of two babies at the same time.

"So, you said you could work from home," she ventured, wanting to find out more about this new Markus. "You're not practicing law anymore?"

He looked up, the tenderness she'd seen on his face when he looked at Phoebe changing to polite tolerance. "I'm in manufacturing."

Liv frowned. "Oh."

She would've been less surprised if he'd said he was studying to be an astronaut. Manufacturing didn't fit him at all. He was a risk taker, a highly charged go-getter who lived life on the edge. Or he had been those things. The things that had made him a world class litigator and had blown their relationship apart.

"I think she's finished." His voice was low. "They need to sleep."

"Of course," Liv said, disappointed he'd changed the subject, but glad the girls would go down for a sleep so they could talk some more.

He stood, and she saw that Zoë had fallen asleep, so she pulled the teat from her perfect little lips, held the baby against her shoulder and then followed him across the room.

They moved down a long, marbled corridor and Liv

suddenly realized what the rich, sweet smell was that she'd noticed as soon as she'd arrived. Vanilla.

She looked outside. Down the length of the glassed corridor sat pots and pots of what she guessed were vanilla orchids, the scent of the shiny green vines filling the house. And it hit her.

A woman had lived here.

Markus had never been interested in plants. And he'd made the comment about a wife. These plants must belong to a woman.

The thought curled through her and she clutched the baby closer. Why did the thought of another woman here with him—sharing his house, his bed—eat at her?

It had been two long years and she couldn't possibly have believed he'd met no one else—the way she hadn't. Yet, to see evidence of another woman's touch here, in his home, his private place, hurt more than she could've imagined.

When the babies were tucked into the wooden cribs that Markus had had delivered, she and Markus both sneaked back to the living room and the sweet danger of being alone with him seeped into Liv's body. Things should be said, ground rules should be established, if they were to survive the next few weeks.

"I have work to do," he said, as she stood by a chair. "If you still want to stay, you can use the apartment at the end of the west wing. Petro's out in the garden protecting small plants from the storm. He'll get you anything you need. I'll go out later and get more supplies for the girls, but I'm sure you'll be fine until I get back." He began to walk toward a door.

Cold shock raced through her. She'd be in charge of the girls alone? "Markus?"

He turned his head but not his whole body. His voice was like starlight, cool and distant. "You need something?"

"You're not going to sit and talk with me so we can work out how we'll do all this?" As she spoke, his eyes darkened. He was keeping as much emotional distance as he could. Protecting himself.

He turned to face her fully, and Liv took the nearest chair, hoping he'd take the hint and sit down, too.

He put both hands low on his hips, defensiveness projecting from every pore. "We've done what we need to do, what we will do until the girls' future is determined. For now, we look after Phoebe and Zoë. That's all."

Liv tried to swallow away the rock in her throat, but in the end she just had to speak through it. "But if we're to do that without tension in the air, we need to talk about things." Did she really mean that? Did she want to go down the gaping hole that was their past?

She'd spent the last two years doing everything in her power to get over him, to believe she'd done the right thing in leaving the way she did. To be here in his house, on his terms, and have to see him every day would be a bigger challenge than she'd expected, but it's what she'd do to prove her love for the girls.

He leaned, strong and rigid, against the arm of the nearest couch, and his proximity started a familiar hum in her chest. At least he was going to keep speaking to her.

"What is there to say, Olivia?" His deep brown irises drew her in. "We had a relationship. You gave up on it. End of story."

"I know I hurt you back then." She lowered her eyes to concentrate on a gold fleck in the marble floor. "And I'm sorry for it. But I made decisions that were right for me at the time."

"Just as you're doing now."

Something in his words disturbed her. Did he think she was putting herself first in wanting the babies?

She clutched the cool silk of her dress and ground it through her fingers. "I came here to claim Phoebe and Zoë, Markus. You never suggested I was completely wasting my time."

Words squeezed directly from her heart—but he needed to see that all she wanted was the next four weeks to be over so she could get on a plane with the girls and leave him behind.

Again, her heart whispered. *Leave him behind again.*

She sat higher in her chair, determined to show him that she'd thought this through, that she was making the right decision this time. "It's my chance to prove my love for Polly and for Phoebe and Zoë."

Her words seemed to move him, soften a small part of his rigid stance.

"Prove your love?" His gaze locked onto hers for a long second before he crossed his arms. "I'd be delighted to see you prove your love for someone. I'd like to believe that you'd always be there for the girls in the good times and bad. That you'd always be there when they needed you. Same city, same country."

His insinuation that she hadn't been there for Polly, that she couldn't settle down, hung in the air.

"My only reference for the way you might behave in the future is the way you've behaved in the past—running when things get difficult, never wanting to put down roots and work at relationships." He paused before finishing with precision. "I need to see who you are before I'll believe you can prove your love."

Desperately, she tried to make a connection with him.

He deserved some explanation as to why she'd left him, why she'd had to leave Paris when she did.

She pulled in a deep breath. She could put love first, and if he knew that, he might be ready to believe she was capable of giving her life to the girls.

"There have been times in my life," she began slowly, her voice catching, "when I haven't always known how to show love. Given my childhood, I've forgiven myself for that."

This was as honest as she could be. Would it be enough for him to understand that she'd changed?

He shifted off the arm of the couch and moved to the window. The wild panorama of churning sea and scurrying clouds framed the tension in his body. "You've been doing a lot of thinking in the last two years."

"This isn't about you and me, Markus; it's about two tiny babies who need to be in the most secure, most loving environment possible."

"You must understand my hesitation in believing you've changed, Liv. Quite simply, you have a history of running out on love when things get tough. And bringing up two babies, night and day, will be tougher than anything else you've run from."

Bile began to inch its way up the back of her throat because he spoke the truth. "You're right," she whispered. "And you need to understand that in doing what I am now, I'm determined to change."

"Determination isn't enough. Two lives are at stake. If you fail, if you run out, even if you tire of being in one place too long, it's the girls who'll pay the price. They're not adults, as I was. I need to be sure you have the capacity to love them the way they deserve to be loved."

He continued, seemingly oblivious to the depths she was

reaching. "I've lived close to the wind, taken some risks and put my life in danger on occasion, but I know true love when I see it. And I don't walk out on it. Just as I won't walk out on Phoebe and Zoë."

He suddenly stopped speaking, and the silence dug into her as she digested his words.

The passion and fire she'd loved all those years ago radiated from him, and she had to fight to push away a deep-seated need to touch him, feel his heat, trace a finger down his jaw . . .

Struggling to keep the emotion from her voice and at the same time bring some calm, she stood. "I think we both need to acknowledge the hurt that's been done in the past and move on from it, Markus."

She could've said different things—that he was the one who'd run off to parachuting weekends in Nice and scuba diving trips off Sardinia. She could've told him how coming home two days late from a caving trip was neither funny nor responsible—that it had scared the life from her and left her alone and lonely. But she didn't. None of that mattered now.

She closed her eyes and bowed her head. She was getting too deep. This was about Phoebe and Zoë, not about them.

She opened her eyes but kept her gaze lowered. "I know love takes determination and sacrifice and commitment, and now I have the opportunity to give those things to the girls. When I'm back with them in Brentwood Bay, I'll be the second-best mother they could ever have."

"And what if you didn't go back to the States?"

She flicked her gaze up to meet his. And she saw a spark of challenge beginning to flame. "What do you mean?"

His jaw tightened but he held her gaze. "What if you

were to stay here and be a part of the girls' lives forever? Allow them to grow up with two people who love them."

"I've told my friends I'll be coming back," she said, confusion at what he was suggesting swimming between her words. "I've said I'll bring the girls back home to a quiet life, and the foster mom I had when I was fourteen wants to help me take care of them."

"You could do that here." His gaze intensified and her heart began to speed. "You could work, visit your fragrance markets when you need to and still be part of the girls' lives. They'd then have a mother and a father."

She shook her head, trying to understand where on earth this idea had come from. "But I'm an American citizen, Markus. I don't have an EU passport. I wouldn't be allowed to stay here."

"You would if you became my wife."

Her eyes grew wide, her lips parted, and her shoulders dropped. His suggestion had had the desired impact.

It might seem uncaring, ruthless even, to make her face the truth in such a blunt way, but Markus wanted to push her, to see how much she'd truly changed, how real her declarations of the last half hour were.

And when she scoffed at his suggestion, as he was certain she would, then she'd show her true colors. She wasn't as prepared to sacrifice everything to put her love for Phoebe and Zoë first as she'd so vehemently insisted.

There was no point in either of them pretending she'd changed, because the bottom line was that he wasn't going to let the girls leave here with someone who didn't know how to prioritize love.

Color had drained from her face. "Your wife?" Her voice trembled before her throat moved in a sharp swallow. "Markus, you can't be serious?"

"Why wouldn't I be?" He breathed a silent sigh of relief that she was as shocked at his proposal as he'd known she'd be. Now she could stop pretending.

"It'd mean you could legally stay here," he said. "Leaving Phoebe and Zoë settled in the only place they know, with the two people in the world who love them, would be the biggest sacrifice you'd ever make." Her eyes were dark and panicked as she chewed on her lip, so he continued. "You talk of wanting to be a mother to them, of proving your love for them. Put them and their needs first. Don't run from here because you can't face me or our past. Stay here so we can raise the girls together."

She held his gaze, her eyes glistening, lip trembling. "You'd marry me? Just so I could stay here? You think you could do that?" she whispered.

So, she was going to humor him for a moment? Okay. But he could carry the challenge through to see her realize, make her really understand, that in refusing him she didn't have what it took to last the distance.

"But you always said marriage was so important to you. I don't understand why you'd do this. How could we make it work?"

Hot memories burned through him. She'd done it again. She'd pulled that string of remembrance that cut deep and reminded him how he'd never had the chance to ask her to marry him before.

He forced himself to continue his charade. "If we're both determined to put the girls first in everything, then of course we could make it work. Couples who've split do it all the time, and if we put the children first in everything, then I

48

don't see why it wouldn't be a success. The girls would remain settled, and they'd have the security and love of two people, not just one."

Even though he made the words sound meaningful and sincere, the immediate vision of having her here permanently, so within his reach and yet so distant, caused him to shiver at even the fantasy of it. A beautiful little family, the sort he'd told her he'd wanted when they'd been together. But she'd always avoided it, saying she wasn't ready to think about it and that the idea of children frightened her.

She sat down hard and held on to the arms of the chair as if steadying herself for a bumpy ride. "It's not something I've considered," she said quietly. "Staying here. I guess I'd just assumed you'd want me to take the girls away, that you wouldn't have room in your life for them the way you didn't have room for things in the past." Her gaze drifted up to his. "But I can see you've changed too."

His chest hollowed. Where was the immediate refusal he'd been expecting? The panic he'd been certain she'd display when she realized he'd called her bluff and really seen through her words? The understanding she'd have no choice but to put her needs first and run again?

She steepled her hands and tapped them on her mouth, but she continued to watch him, her eyes steady. "I can see how me staying here would give the girls what they need, Markus, but surely it's not something you'd be comfortable with?"

He pulled his shoulders back. "I'm committed to making decisions that wholly benefit Phoebe and Zoë. My needs don't come into the equation. If what's best for them means sharing their care with you, then of course that's something I'd do."

"But what would it give you?"

As she sat in that chair, her fingers touching the lips he'd kissed so many times, he couldn't believe what he was hearing. And the remnants of long-buried desire began to unfurl inside. The way a tiny frown grazed the smooth skin of her forehead, the way she rolled her teeth between her lips, they both made him want to put all this right, forget what had happened in the past and just drag her into his arms.

You, he wanted to say*, it would give me the you I've dreamed about. Your face to look at. Your laugh to listen to.*

Having you here would give me back you. And the part of me that died when you walked away from me. From us. From our love.

"It would give me a chance to stay in the girls' lives. I've been with them night and day and I can't imagine giving them up."

"You wouldn't consider moving back to the States?"

Her gaze held him and he couldn't pull his away. "I'd consider whatever was the right decision for the girls. They were born here and are citizens. I've made a commitment to my family to run the business here. And Cyprus is closer to your European markets than living back home."

"If I thought it would work, I might consider it." Her voice had steadied.

Words sat paralyzed in his throat. She was really considering this? Really believed they could put their past behind them for the sake of the girls? And despite it being a ridiculous idea, and that all the problems of the past would be magnified a hundred times with two babies in their care, he let the vision carry him away for a moment and held the gaze she trapped him with.

4

*M*arkus knew he'd been longer than he should've when he swung the car through the large iron gates at the bottom of the driveway and made the journey over the hill to his house. The moon shone bright after the storm, and the air was still and sticky. The local store hadn't had the brand of formula the girls preferred, so he'd had to drive all the way into the town of Paphos to get what he needed. It was after ten, and he hoped the babies hadn't woken and that Liv hadn't had to cope on her own.

As the car came over the brow of the hill, his stomach dropped.

The house was lit like a beacon. Every room on every level glowed, illuminating the surrounding garden.

Exhaustion from nights of broken sleep, mixed with the knowledge that he'd be spending the night under the same roof as Liv, sat heavy across his shoulders. He got out of the car and rushed up the steps.

This was not a happy light.

He gripped the handle and then pushed the door open,

the silence surprising him, and he let out the breath he hadn't known he'd been holding. Perhaps the babies were being fed?

His housekeeper, Petro, stood in the middle of wall-to-wall mess, but Liv and the babies were nowhere to be seen.

"Thank God!" Petro exclaimed in Greek, before marching toward him and dumping a pile of baby clothes in his arms. "She's no good this new nanny! You have to fire her. She knows nothing about feeding or changing or how to get those angel babies to sleep. This is all too much, Markus. When I agreed to this situation, I didn't expect it—"

"Okay, Petro, okay." Markus dropped the clothes on the couch and put a hand on Petro's shaking shoulder. The poor guy. Markus hadn't told him the whole story yet, so he'd assumed Liv was the nanny. He was such a perfectionist and ran such a strict household with everything in its place—this would be very stressful for him. "You go home. We can take care of this in the morning, and when you're back, we'll have a talk about all of this."

Petro threw up his hands. "You cannot wake up to a mess like this! I will not allow it! I do not believe this woman knows how to take care of a household. No, I will stay and put things in order. Just make sure she doesn't come near me! She doesn't even speak Greek!" He finished in disgust.

The older man continued picking up bags and bottles, and Markus couldn't hold back a small grin. There was never any point arguing with Petro. "Where is Olivia?"

His housekeeper waved a hand in the direction of the east wing. "In with the babies. I think one's asleep, thank God! They've been crying since you left! They are such beautiful little things and deserve to have someone take care of them who knows what she's doing!"

As Markus stole quietly up the corridor, the knowledge

of Liv struggling with the girls while he was gone sent a bolt of guilt through him. He knew how hard it was, being alone with two babies, the feelings of panic and inadequacy, and this was all so new for her.

He hoped it hadn't been as bad as Petro had described.

Everything was silent as he stood by the babies' bedroom door. A single lamp sent a cozy butter glow across the room, but his gaze stalled on the form of Liv, in a rocking chair, her lips moving in a whisper to the bundle in her arms. The power and the beauty of it sent a grip of want to his soul, and he quickly stepped back into the shadows so she wouldn't see him.

Her deep gold curls fell in messy ringlets around her shoulders, and the rhythm of her rocking caused them to move and glint in the light. She'd always been beautiful, but it wasn't her face or her body that touched him deeply now, it was the calm, gentle way she rocked and whispered, rocked and whispered, as if she poured her heart and soul into the child in her arms.

Sorrow ran swift through his veins—sorrow that it was precisely this patience, this taking time in love, that she'd denied him in the past. In the end, it had been her desire not to stop running, not to show her deepest love, that had changed his world forever.

He'd loved this woman. With his heart and soul and breath, he'd loved this woman. And she'd left him without looking back.

The fact she was now so obviously capable of dropping everything for someone she felt strongly about made him wonder if everything she'd said this afternoon, everything she'd promised, might be true after all.

But he couldn't allow himself to hope.

She looked up, her eyes heavy, exhaustion evident in her slow movements. "Markus. Is that you?" she whispered.

He stepped out confidently, as if he'd just arrived, instead of watching her every move. "I'm sorry I took so long."

"It's okay," she said softly. "I've been trying to imagine what it'd be like if I had to look after the girls on my own." She stood and carefully placed the baby in the crib next to her sister's. "I would never have imagined it'd be so exhausting."

He watched as she leaned over to tuck the soft pink blankets under the mattress, and then she straightened and turned to him. "It makes me realize what you've been through."

The softness in her eyes sweetened the bitterness he'd tasted a moment ago, and he couldn't bring himself to look away from it. The longer she held his stare, the quicker his pulse became at his temples. Finally, she turned back to the crib. "Can you believe how gorgeous they look when they're asleep?"

She was stunning. Despite the way her shoulders sagged from exhaustion and her hair sat wildly about her shoulders —in fact, because of those things, and because she was doing what she'd said she would, being here and constant and responsible for Phoebe and Zoë—Markus wanted to turn her to him and lose himself in her kiss and her body as he'd done so many times before.

He took a step forward, wanting to tell her what seeing her like this meant to him.

Rubbing her small hands across her eyes, she said, "I'm going to bed. I asked Petro to move me closer to the babies so I can hear them in the night." She pointed out the open door and across the hallway to the blue room, the one right next to the master bedroom. "I hope you don't mind."

His pulse spiked. She couldn't stay there, only inches from his own bed. He'd put her in the west wing for a reason. To keep him away from temptation and trouble. It was enough that she was in his house, but to think of her lying warm in sleep—only the sheerest negligee covering her milky skin—was too much for his vivid imagination.

"You don't need to move. I'll do the night feeds," he said. "I've got a routine worked out where I have the bottles ready, and when one baby wakes, I wake the other so I only get up once, twice at the most. You've done enough already, and I don't need to go out to work tomorrow. We can move your things back to the other room then."

Again, she looked directly into his eyes, and the connection sent a jolt of deep familiarity to his heart. "I want to do this together, Markus. I really do. We'll be able to get the feeding done faster if we do it together, and I want you to show me what you've learned. You've spent enough time doing this on your own. I'm here to help now."

Smile lines bracketed her mouth. She wasn't shutting him out, wasn't trying to take complete control. He touched her arm and the shock of feeling her body again, warm and delicate, sent waves of desire pulsing through him. "Thank you for doing this," he said. "Thank you for being here."

She leaned toward him slightly. "I'd do anything for the girls." And with her words, he was shunted back to reality. She hadn't come here for him; this wasn't the fantasy he'd dreamed of. Liv was here for Phoebe and Zoë, nothing more, and he had to keep remembering that.

They both turned as Petro came into the hallway and loudly opened and shut a linen closet without looking at them.

"I did what you said," Liv said to the older man, and he peered slowly around the door. "I rocked them both in the chair and they eventually fell asleep."

Petro muttered something and moved toward her with a pile of clean wraps. "You might need these in the night," he said gruffly, before turning and walking back down the hallway.

"Don't mind him," Markus said as he gently guided her into the blue room. "I haven't explained everything to him yet. He's become very protective of the girls and will be wondering what you're doing here. I'll explain who you are tomorrow."

He switched on a lamp and led her to the bed; her suitcase sat, unopened, at the end of it.

"He pretended he didn't speak English for a long time," Liv said, a grin tugging at her cheek. "It was only after we couldn't settle the girls that he gave me his piece of advice."

"He'll come around. We'll sort out a routine for the girls tomorrow. You're exhausted and need some sleep. I'll go and get their bottles ready now, so when they wake in the night, we'll be ready."

Liv touched a weary hand to her face, and he could see she was almost asleep already. "You'll call me when they cry?"

"I promise. Now get some sleep, and I'll wake you when I need to."

He closed her door with a soft click. The perfect metaphor for the barriers that sat so firmly between them.

5

A hearty cry split the early morning quiet. The clock showed 5:15 a.m. as Liv dragged herself from a dreamless sleep, clawing her way to the surface when she remembered where she was.

She felt like she'd been awake all night, reliving the moment Markus had asked her to marry him. In the past, she'd fantasized about that moment and the way he'd hold her in his arms and pour out his deep love for her with his words. But his recent proposal left a cavernous hole in her heart. Nothing like the way she'd reacted to his fantasy proposal in her dreams.

He was being practical, logical, and the fact he could ask her and not understand the anguish, the burning sadness it caused inside her, made Liv realize he'd truly moved on. He'd never have suggested it if he still cared.

What it did show her, though, was the lengths he'd go to provide for the tiny babies in his care, and that knowledge unsettled her.

He'd admitted he wasn't their father, and yet he was still prepared to stop her trying to take them away. Well, a marriage wouldn't solve their problems. His solution would never work. Being near him every day, waiting until he did something dangerous, would bring her a lifetime of heartache. He knew Polly had been her best friend, that it would have been Liv she'd want to care for her babies. Why couldn't he accept that?

She threw back the covers, swung her legs out of bed and then pushed her feet into flip-flops. She wasn't ready to think about how she'd explain all that to him. Last night she'd pretended she was considering it because "are you completely crazy" hadn't seemed polite in the circumstances. She'd wait until the moment was right to say no.

"You're on!" Markus's tousled head appeared around her door, his eyes hazy with sleep, and on reflex Liv reached for her robe. "They slept eight hours. Must have been exhausted."

He disappeared again, and she took a moment to breathe—to banish the thudding in her chest at seeing him in his achingly familiar, mussed-up morning state. She'd never have dreamed this situation—this intimacy—would ever happen again.

Both babies were crying. She hurried into their room just as Markus picked up a tiny bundle. She lifted the other and felt warm baby breaths against her neck. Immediately, both girls quietened. Markus turned to her and smiled long and slow. "Maybe we're getting the hang of this."

It was *that* smile, the one she'd carried inside her for so long. The one that had made her feel she was the center of his world.

She followed him down the hallway, trying to avoid watching the way his T-shirt rode up a little over his cotton pajama pants. Maybe this was some cruel punishment—to have to be in the same house as him, to work together and have all of him within touching distance.

The living room was cloaked in the golden glow of a rain-washed dawn, and Liv paused in amazement at the clean-up job Petro must have done last night. "How long has Petro been your housekeeper?" she asked, as Markus moved to the kitchen and retrieved bottles from the fridge.

Since your girlfriend moved out? Since your wife left?

"Since I've been back in Cyprus," he said. "He's normally with me in the city house but comes here with me in the summer. He does the gardens too. He worked for my grandparents when they lived here."

Liv sat and checked a little toe to confirm she was holding Phoebe, then gave the tiny baby a slow cuddle, the closeness calming her. "Gardening? Yes, I noticed your vanilla orchids out there. Do you harvest them or does someone like the flowers?"

Markus placed Zoë on his shoulder and patted her back as he waited for the milk to warm. "Did you sleep well?" he asked. She glanced at him. Was he avoiding her questions?

"Not so well. I was awake for a long time." She'd try another tack. "What else do you grow apart from orchids?"

His face was impassive. "Roses, lavender, orange, lemon, lime, pistachio, hazelnut."

What? He'd never been interested in gardening. A sudden pall of sadness filled her chest. She didn't really know him anymore. A person could do so much in two years. A person could completely change.

The knowledge of what she'd lost with him crept into her thoughts again, as it often did when she was over tired. Things could have been so different if she hadn't been called away, if he'd been more reliable, if . . .

She gave herself a mental shake. There was no point

thinking like this. The past was the past. Since the news about Polly, Liv had vowed to focus on her future with Phoebe and Zoë, on taking them back to the States as Polly would've wished.

And what about Markus? Can you abandon him again?

She watched him take the bottle of milk from the hot water.

If I don't love him, I can't abandon him. If he doesn't love me, there's nothing to abandon.

She shook her head to remove the rogue thoughts. "You grow all of those things in your own garden?"

"The milk's ready."

Okay, so he *was* avoiding her questions and, perhaps, letting her know he wanted to keep his private life private.

She looked out at the brightening Mediterranean and sighed as she let the beauty of her surroundings wash over her. "This is such a magical place."

When they were once again sitting opposite each other, ready to feed the babies as they'd done the day before, Liv had the sudden image of the next few weeks stretching out in an unchanging routine that would only get more and more familiar. The thought both frightened and thrilled her. If she wanted to make sure she didn't develop feelings for Markus again, the easiest way would be to make sure she was around him as little as possible.

"You don't really need to stay away from work, you know." She gave Phoebe the bottle, and the baby sucked hungrily, her tiny fists waving in the air. "Once I learn their routine, I'm sure I'll be fine with the feeding. The book I was reading last night said they should sleep most of the time in the first few weeks anyway."

He'd done her a favor in leaving her alone for so long last night. Although it had been stressful, the fact she'd had to go through the process by herself meant she was much more confident in her ability to organize the girls' feeds alone. And that old fear of having children, and of being responsible for the lives of others, had been dampened a little.

"It makes sense that I help you out," he said. "The girls are used to me now. It's not a chore." His eyes, which were soft when he gazed at Zoë, shuttered when they swung to look at her.

Liv tried to sound brighter than she felt. "You could pop home a couple of times a day from your work, and you could do the bathing at night."

Every minute she could wrest from him, every second she could negotiate that they spent apart, was necessary for her sanity, and if she were truthful, to protect her fragile hold on her treacherous emotions. If he wasn't in her line of sight every minute, she might not find her mind running away on itself, creating scenarios as it was now. How they could work together to raise the girls . . .

He didn't meet her eyes, focusing instead on Zoë in his arms. "I'll be staying here. I can work when the girls sleep."

He still wanted to watch what she was doing with the girls.

"What sort of manufacturing can you do from home?" As soon as she'd said it and his gaze snapped up to meet hers, she knew she was pushing him, moving too close, but something in her wanted to know.

"*Loukoumi*."

The word made no sense to her. "I'm sorry . . .?"

"We manufacture *loukoumi*, Turkish delight."

The scent of lemon, the smell of hazelnuts in his office. Of course! And then heat spread through her as something else made sense. The vanilla orchids. They were all his.

"How lovely. Wasn't that your grandparents' business? With your sense of taste and smell, you must love it." She couldn't help the smile that pressed into her cheeks.

They'd shared a love of smells and tastes in France—so perfect for her perfume studies. Whether it was a cinnamon stick at a street stall, a ripe piece of cheese at a local market, or the scent of salt spray in Gascony, their lives had been one sensual experience after the other.

"It's okay." He shrugged, and the soft cotton of his T-shirt rippled across his wide shoulders. "I took over when my grandfather died."

"It's the perfect job for you. You love wine, coffee, food and . . . the texture of Turkish delight is so mmmmm . . ."

She froze. His gaze had grown more distant as she'd listed her intimate knowledge of him. A strong hand of regret tightened around her throat. She'd said too much, become too close, and he was locking her out, making her very aware she was unwelcome in that part of his life.

A small crease touched his brow and his eyes slowly tracked her face, his midnight pupils growing larger. "I don't seem to taste things the way I used to or be able to differentiate the subtleties of one smell from another. Things've been different in the last two years." He didn't look down in shame or anger but held her stare.

"Maybe it just takes practice." She dipped her chin and pretended to focus on straightening Phoebe's blanket.

She needed to step away from the familiarity of this conversation—avoid this type of connection with Markus—and get back to the impersonal nature of routine.

But she made the mistake of looking up at him.

From the lick of dark hair that fell haphazardly across his forehead, to the way his strong hands held the baby in his arms, she took in the whole of him. Her skin tingled at memories of his body under her hands—the way his muscle, rendered hard from skiing, rock climbing, surfing, sat taut like the strings of a fine and familiar instrument.

And then something snapped deep inside her—maybe the wall she'd erected two years ago, maybe the shield that had existed since she was a lonely little girl, but whatever it was exposed a deep, beating part of her—and made her want to reach out to him. "Maybe you need to believe you can feel those things again and the old sensations might return."

As soon as the words were out, with her heart hammering in her chest, Liv knew she hadn't been talking about taste or smell but rather about something they both knew far more intimately instead.

"Good morning, Mr. Panos, it's Ana-Maria Clerides," a voice said in English, the round vowels of a Canadian accent cushioning the words.

"This is not Mr. Panos," Petro replied. "I will fetch him for you." He pulled the phone receiver from his ear, but a muffled "Oh" made him listen again, and this time she spoke in Greek. "Then you must be Mr. Pantazis, the house-keeper," the woman said, her tone more serious.

Petro cast a look through to the living room where Liv was folding washing and continued in English. "I've been practicing my English a lot lately." Two English-speaking women in two days? He hoped the one on the end of the phone wasn't going to be employed here as well. Markus had asked to speak to him this morning but then he'd been called away suddenly. Liv was pleasant enough, with her soft smile and bright eyes, but she seemed to know very little about baby care. "I'm quite good at giving instructions for things like boiling water and folding washing," he said.

The beginnings of a chuckle could be heard before it was stifled.

"We can speak in Greek if you prefer."

"I'm sorry, who is this?" he asked, again in English

"I'm the social worker in charge of the twin girls."

"Ah."

Those poor, poor babies. He'd never met their mother. Markus had said she was an old friend from his home town in California, and that he had to take care of her babies after she died. He'd wondered if the girls were Markus's daughters, but Markus hadn't brought a woman to either his city house or the house at Aphrodite's rock in the whole time he'd been back from Paris.

Petro was old school. He didn't ask until he was told. And he trusted his employer completely. If Markus wanted him to have more detail about the girls, then he'd tell him. It made sense that he'd employed Liv as the girls' nanny, though. She spoke English, like their mother, and seemed to have known Markus for some time.

"I'm coming to see how the babies are doing in a couple of weeks, and I wondered if I could ask you a few questions."

"Me?"

"You're employed at the house where the girls are staying, aren't you?" Her tone was gentler.

"I am. I'm Mr. Panos's housekeeper at both his residences." He took the phone into the study and sat down. Why was a social worker interested in him? To find out if he was a suitable person to be around Phoebe and Zoë? "I raised four children on my own when my wife died in her early thirties," he said. "I cook and clean and can change

64

diapers. I've offered to stay and help Markus with the night feeds, but he says both of us shouldn't be sleep deprived."

"Mr. Pantazis—"

"Petro."

"Petro, I'm not questioning your suitability as a member of the household."

"Good, because there are some members of this household who should have learned how to do some of those things in nanny school, or at least her mother should have shown her. I made sure all my children knew how to cook and clean before they left home, the girls *and* the boys. Now, people pay good money for nannies who don't know the basics." Only yesterday, Liv had put a red sweater in the wash with all the girls' clothes that he liked to keep white. He'd been horrified when everything came out pink, but Liv had thought it hilarious.

There was silence at the end of the line, and Petro tapped a fist against his forehead. *Rats*. He shouldn't have said all that. Liv might be the most hopeless example of a nanny he'd ever seen, but he could see she cared deeply about those babies already, and he didn't want to get her into trouble.

"There's a nanny in the house too? I wasn't aware of that. Could I have her name, please?"

This conversation was going from bad to worse.

"Olivia's only new," he said quickly. "She's American, which is good because the girls' mother was American, so they'll respond to her accent. She'll learn how to do everything else. It must be difficult for her being in a new country, too."

"By Olivia, do you mean Ms. Bailey? The woman who's applied to take the girls back to America?"

Petro's mouth fell open. "She's taking them away from Markus? Why would she do that?"

Questions dipped and dived inside his brain, and Petro could hear Ana-Maria dragging in a breath.

"I'm sorry, Petro. I shouldn't have—"

"There's no need for you to apologize," he said gruffly. "Maybe my English isn't as good as I thought it was because all of this is news to me."

"It's been a very busy time and things have moved very quickly," Ana-Maria said. "I'm sure Mr. Panos will tell you everything in time. He knows you need to undergo our good character checks also."

"How long will you need to interview me?" Petro asked, already planning what he was going to say to Markus about letting him think Liv was the nanny.

"Thirty minutes should do it." Ana-Maria's voice was brighter, but it didn't sound natural. "I'll be at the house longer than that, of course—interviewing Mr. Panos and Ms. Bailey."

"I hope you'll have time to stay for some afternoon tea," Petro said as he moved out of the study and looked toward Markus's office. "It's always better to discuss things over a piece of cake."

Though she was still tired, a strange feeling of contentment settled over Liv as she enjoyed the routine of looking after the girls. To have uncapped some of the bottled emotion between her and Markus felt good, but his proposal sat like a heavy weight between them. She hadn't mentioned it again, and he hadn't asked for her reply. All she could focus on right now was looking after the girls minute by minute.

After feeding and changing the girls and putting them back down, Markus had taken an urgent Zoom call in his office, and she was glad of the time apart if only to stop the growing desire to be near him.

Late morning, the phone rang in the foyer. She heard Petro answer it and forgot about it until, stone-faced, he walked over to where she sat folding washing and handed her the phone.

"It's for you," he said briskly, not meeting her gaze. "Where is Markus? I need to speak to him."

Confused and instantly curious why anyone would want to speak with her, Liv nodded in the direction of the office wing. "He said he had an urgent call." Petro glowered, harrumphed, and marched off.

"Hello?"

"Ms. Bailey?" Liv's gut curled in response to a woman's voice. Was it his mother? A girlfriend?

"It's Ana-Maria Clerides. I'm calling to let you know I'll be making a home visit next Tuesday. It's important we see the girls' needs are being met, and that Mr. Panos and you are managing to care for them appropriately. I've also booked the girls in for a medical check with a doctor appointed by the Service for Families and Children. It's on the fifteenth."

"Of course," Liv said, relieved it was the social worker. She started as Petro marched from the office, flung open the French doors and stormed out, with Markus in hot pursuit.

"I'll want to see the girls of course, but I'd like to interview you and Mr. Panos both separately and together. I've also spoken to Mr. Panos's housekeeper, and I'll want to interview him as well."

Liv sat straighter in the chair. Judging by Petro's reaction to the telephone call and speaking to Markus, Markus had just told him the whole story and he was not happy about being dragged into it. Another thought struck her like a hammer to her chest.

Petro didn't like her. That was obvious. When it had only been him and her with the babies yesterday, he'd huffed and puffed and hardly said a word. How would that affect the way he spoke about her to Ana-Maria? A shiver rippled up her spine. Would Petro do *anything* to protect Markus?

She took the details for the girls' doctor appointment from Ana-Maria, said goodbye, and hurried out onto the deck. Shielding her eyes from the sun, she could see Markus and Petro standing partway down the hill among the lavender, the older man gesticulating his arms as he talked. Liv sat straight-backed on the luxurious outdoor couch and chewed her lip, as indecision and fatigue washed through her.

A few minutes later, Petro stormed back up the hill and past her into the house, but not before she caught the look he shot her. Was it her tired imagination or did she see a thaw in those hard eyes? He stalked into the kitchen then started pulling out pots and pans, opening and closing cupboards.

Liv turned as Markus walked toward her. Lines of concern bracketed his mouth.

"You've told him everything?" she whispered as she stood and met him halfway on the sweeping deck.

"I have now. I should've done it first thing this morning, but there was a problem with my American distributor, and I had to schedule a quick meeting."

"He seems pretty angry." She glanced back to the kitchen, worry dancing up her body

"He's embarrassed that he thought you were the nanny. Now I've told him everything, he's probably cooking up an apology dinner for being so hard on you." He rubbed a hand across his face, and she was moved by the weary look in his eyes. Maybe he hadn't slept either.

"But it's not his fault. He didn't know."

Markus huffed out a breath. "Of course, it isn't. It's mine. Ana-Maria wanted details of anyone else who lived here. I told her about Petro, and she said she'd need to talk with him, so I should have made telling him a priority."

"And you hadn't told him he might be questioned?" She bit her lip.

Markus shook his head. "I should've told him what was going on, but I know how passionate he gets. All he knew was that the babies' mother was an old friend of mine, and when she died, they had no one else to take care of them."

He looked at her then, really looked at her with eyes that spoke of certainty—and the power of what he'd said struck her between the ribs.

No one would be the winner here. The longer she stayed with the custody issues unresolved, the more people would be affected, and the harder things would become. Not least of all because every time Markus stood in front of her as he did now, confident and sure, espresso-colored eyes flashing, she had to dampen down the need for him that kept blooming, unbidden, from deep within.

She swallowed away the want and the guilt and thought of the one foster family she'd stayed in touch with.

Now, she had the opportunity to provide the same sort of loving environment for Phoebe and Zoë, and that had to be her motivation for everything. She had to make firm decisions now, hard ones, but always with the girls' welfare paramount.

Markus leaned against the side of the house. "It'd be best if we left him alone for a while."

Liv had to shake off the thoughts that were growing heavier in her mind to concentrate on what he was saying. "Yes, of course."

"Let's take the girls for a walk down to the beach. Petro can have some time by himself to digest what I've told him."

She had to stop her hand from flying to her mouth as she imagined them together, just like old times. All she could think about was how, in the past, they'd strolled along beaches, his strong, protective arm holding her close against his hard body, and her hand inching up under his T-shirt . . .

"I can manage," she said on a hot breath. "It's really only me he needs time away from."

"I want to come." Markus's gaze rested on her fingers nervously stroking her lips and he grinned. "We need to give that flash new stroller a test drive anyway."

Her skin chilled. It wasn't that he wanted to spend time with her; he wanted to present a united front to Ana-Maria. Now that Petro was to be interviewed, Markus would want to pretend everything was fine between them.

She could do it. Of course, she could. It might break some of the ice, or cool some of the heat, depending on which way you looked at things . . . and she *needed* the heat cooled.

When they had the girls strapped into the stroller and rugged up against the sea breeze, they set off down a path that led from the house to the beach. Rows of lavender surrounded them, the heads of deep purple, lilac and mauve nodding in the light wind.

Liv breathed in a lungful of the sweet fragrance combined with the tangy coastal air, and a layer of tension slipped from her shoulders. Beyond the lavender was a stand of orange trees and, closer to the beach, another of what looked like almonds. The teasing scent of all three filled her head.

"Do you use these in your Turkish Delight?" she asked as she walked behind Markus, who was pushing the stroller. The broad expanse of his back was covered in a simple black T-shirt, and muscles stretched and recovered as he maneuvered past rocks and bushes.

He glanced over his shoulder and shot her a wry look. "That was the idea."

She frowned. "What do you mean?"

"When I moved here from Paris, I had the crazy idea I could formulate my own essences, try out some new combinations. I imagined I'd have a cottage laboratory where I'd get back to basics. The company's become hugely successful because of our great marketing, but I wanted to bring some honesty back to it." He paused to negotiate some rocks with the stroller before continuing. "I moved my grandfather's old still into the workshop out back of the house." His shoulders stiffened. "It hasn't come to anything."

Liv thought back to the conversation they'd had about his senses being diminished. He'd hinted his lack of feeling had something to do with their break up and part of her understood what he meant. "You seem more settled," she ventured, "as if you don't need to race around doing all the crazy things you used to. Do you still fly?" From somewhere, the question she'd most wanted to ask had come hurtling out of her mouth, and she didn't know if she was ready to hear his answer.

He stopped, stood statue-still, and her heart dropped like a stone down a well. All the old feelings of desperation, worry, fear that she might lose him the way she'd lost her parents came roaring back to life. She tripped on a piece of hard ground but recovered.

He turned to look at her and then down to where she'd tripped. "Are you okay?"

The concern on his face was obvious, the light in his eyes one she'd studied a hundred times. She waved him on and then looked out to sea to avoid his gaze, not wanting him to see the emotion that was surely plastered on her face.

She had to know if he was still putting himself at risk by doing the extreme sport and rescue helicopter work that had scared the living daylights out of her.

The thought that he could die the way her parents had and leave the girls alone had been with her since she'd arrived. She couldn't bear to think of the girls losing another person who loved them.

Shoving her hands in her pockets, she walked past him so she didn't have to meet his gaze. Not wanting him to guess how desperate she was for his answer, she tried to shift the conversation. "This place is breathtaking." Sun-sparkles off the sea winked conspiratorially, as if she wasn't the only one who knew how her heart beat raggedly hoping he'd changed.

When one of the girls began to fuss, Liv turned around.

"I don't fly anymore," he said.

As small lines pulled together on his forehead and a shadow passed across his face, relief threatened to erupt out of her.

"Just the flying, or all those other things?" she asked, her voice faltering. "The diving, the BASE jumping, the rock climbing?"

"Everything."

She couldn't believe it. He'd stopped doing the things she hadn't been able to live with? Stopped taking the risks that had made her so determined to take the girls from him?

One baby was now crying, and Markus pushed the buggy back and forth.

The suddenness of his answer scrambled her thoughts. Where did that leave her resolve, her determination to take the girls away?

"I didn't think you'd ever give those things up," she said, desperate to know why he'd stopped, why he'd finally turned his back on what had destroyed them. "Especially after I asked you to give them up so many times and you didn't."

He took a step toward her and something pulled deep in her chest. As he dragged a hand across his jaw, her eyes were drawn there, and she remembered the way those fingers felt on her skin, dancing their way across her body, leaving her gasping for him. Feelings that had never gone away. Feelings that were with her in the drugged moment of first waking and in the threadlike connection to reality before she fell asleep. Every. Day.

"I have a responsibility to the girls," he said as the wail became louder. "I will protect them and keep them safe, and I can't guarantee that if I'm doing something risky." He looked into the stroller, his face grim. "I don't want to do those things anymore because now I understand what they could cost me."

He tilted his head, as if waiting for her to say something, but she couldn't.

"Look, perhaps we should head back," he said. "She might need changing."

The thought that he finally understood, finally realized why she'd asked him to give those things up before, was bittersweet. He was doing everything she'd asked, living his life responsibly and safely, only now she wasn't the most important person in his life, and he wasn't doing it for her.

73

6

*M*arkus was concerned at how unsettled the girls were. In the past few days, nothing seemed to pacify Phoebe and Zoë. A quick glance at the clock showed him it was fast approaching midnight. Fatigue mixed with trepidation tracked down his spine.

Before Petro had left for the day, he'd cooked Markus and Liv dinner, which they'd shoveled down while standing with a baby over each of their shoulders, something that had become routine in the week that Liv had been here. Now, they'd fed and changed the girls again and were trying to put them back to bed.

Markus had no idea what was wrong. The girls had slept most of the day and early evening in the first few weeks while he'd gained skills as a parent, but now they were more wakeful, harder to settle, and his newfound confidence was slipping away.

Had he messed with their routine in bringing them to Aphrodite's Rock? He'd been hoping they were comfortable having two caregivers now. But above everything, he hoped Phoebe and Zoë weren't picking up on his uncertainty about Liv. He had to ensure they felt protected and loved.

"Do you think it's wind?" Liv asked. She turned anxious, troubled eyes in his direction as she jiggled Phoebe in a front pack. A nearly full moon made the sea silver through the picture windows, and it was as if the four of them were the only people awake in the world.

Liv paced backward and forward across the room, exhaustion lines hugging her eyes as she dodged rugs and wipes, bottles and wraps that were strewn everywhere. Such a contrast to the way the house had before two tiny bundles had turned their worlds upside down.

She was dressed in loose pants and a T-shirt and had her ringlets tied back in a low ponytail, although as the evening wore on more and more strands had come loose. And she'd never looked lovelier.

"One of those books you suggested said wind can give them stomach pain and until you can work the bubble out from their tummy they won't settle," she said, her voice laced with concern.

Both girls were fine when they were carried, but the second they were put down they'd start crying again, building to a symphony in stereo that buried itself in his brain and turned his nerve fibers raw.

Although the books said the babies would spend some time crying when they were put down, a string of unease pulled taut every time Markus thought either of them were upset.

"Could be." He stopped pacing and rubbed his hand up and down the pink cotton of Zoë's nightgown, the feel of the fragile body beneath startling him as it did every time one of the girls was in his arms. The downy tufts of hair on her head tickled his chin as she nodded into him, and he breathed in the baby scent that was like nothing else he'd ever experienced. "Or maybe it's a growth spurt. My book says they can have one of those when they might want to feed all day and all night."

He watched as Liv walked up and down with Phoebe's tiny face snuggled into the creamy skin of her neck, and he felt the now familiar burst of warmth when he watched her with one of the twins. She'd smell of jasmine and rose water on her neck there—he remembered from when his face had been buried in that same place ...

In his wildest dreams, he'd never have imagined she'd be like this with babies. When they'd been in Paris, he'd told her he couldn't wait to have children with her. A family as soon as possible. But every time he'd mentioned it, she'd shut him down, shut him out, and now seeing the capacity for love she displayed every day brought a chilling reminder of what he'd lost when Liv walked out.

"We could've had this," he whispered. Fatigue played some funny tricks, and he'd said aloud the words he'd meant to keep to himself. "Do you ever stop and think that our child would be five now? If we'd had a family when I'd wanted to start one."

She turned; her eyes glassy. "I know, Markus. But it wasn't right, not the right circumstances."

"These are pretty incredible circumstances too," he said, trying to sound light but wanting her to think through his question.

She walked past without meeting his gaze. "Now it's not about what you and I might want, it's about what Phoebe and Zoë need. It's completely different."

He forced a deep breath. The girls' grizzles were the only sound in the room.

Get back on track, Markus. Focus on two tiny babies who need you.

"I guess we'll just have to keep walking until they're asleep." He threw her a grin. "One thing that'll come out of all this is we're both going to be fit. I'm sure this floor's getting a track worn into it."

The exhausted smile she threw back at him was so sweet he could taste it. Her cheeks were tinged pink, her face without makeup, and she'd never looked more beautiful. "Fit and with great muscle tone from lifting these precious weights up and down. I can feel my biceps getting bigger by the day."

"Me too," he said. "And every now and then I get a whiff of myself and it's all sour milk and baby wipes. Who needs perfume when you can smell like this all day for free." He chuckled.

Liv laughed and then caught his eye before she paced past. "Do you think about what they'll be like?" she said, startling him by talking about a time in the future neither of them had acknowledged. "When they're older. I can see they're going to have Polly's huge brown eyes and her gorgeous eyelashes, but I wonder what they'll be like as people."

"I bet they'll laugh like Polly used to," he said as he rubbed Zoë's back in circles. He remembered with warmth how Liv's live-wire friend had lived life at full throttle. The three of them grew up in Brentwood Bay, but he met Polly through Liv when he and Liv began dating at eighteen. "And maybe have that way of looking at you like Polly did, as if you were the only person in the world." He thought about the girls as teenagers, as young women, and something powerful swept over him. "But I guess it depends on what sort of upbringing they have."

Liv eased herself gingerly into a chair, her loose ringlets moving across her shoulders. "What would you like for them?" She looked up at him, an openness that he hadn't seen from her in a long time shining in her eyes.

Phoebe let out a squawk as she realized she'd stopped moving, but as soon as Liv was settled and holding the little girl in her arms, Liv rubbed Phoebe's back once more and the crying stopped. "I mean, what do you really want them to experience growing up? The sort of upbringing you had, or something different?"

Markus held Zoë close, her tiny heart beating against his chest. Liv was opening a door to a path they'd never journeyed down, and the promise of it was too much for him to refuse. He took the chair next to her, cocooning Zoë in his arms and rocking her.

"To be loved," he said quietly. "To always know they are loved and accepted no matter what they do, or who they are with. To know that someone, somewhere, loves them unconditionally."

Liv's gaze lifted to his and the joy in her luminous violet eyes connected directly with his heart. The warmth of their bond, a shared purpose they'd never really had before, wrapped itself around him like a warm sweater on a winter's day.

Her face glowed as she put a hand over her mouth to stifle a yawn. "And that they'll always have a home, somewhere they feel safe and protected. That's got to be the greatest gift a parent can give a child. I think about all the things I missed out on growing up in care."

Despite her obvious exhaustion, her cheeks were flushed with memories, and a burst of pain flared in his chest. She wanted all the things for Phoebe and Zoë that she'd searched for when she'd tried to find her place in the world.

"I want them to play a musical instrument too," she continued, the spark in her eyes growing. "Maybe the violin."

Markus grinned. "Or the bagpipes?"

Liv laughed so loudly and suddenly that Phoebe let out a wail, and Liv tut-tutted as she rocked her closer. "Oh, sorry, sweetie," she said. Her gaze met his again, a happy glow radiating from her. "Can you imagine? Two little five-year-olds with pigtails, sawing backward and forward on a violin, or marching in a band playing their pipes, and us loving every minute of it!"

He held her gaze, and when she bit her lip, he knew she'd been imagining them together with the girls. He didn't know what to do with the thought, so he stowed it away for later.

"Or maybe it'll be sports and we'll have to drag ourselves out of bed for 5 a.m. swim training, or soccer in the winter," he said to break the spell her gaze had over him.

She blew out a soft breath before looking down again. "Where they grow up will have a huge impact on them. On their sense of belonging, of being loved."

"We can give that to them in either country," he said. "If you and I share their care, we can give them all those things, that stability, that soft place to fall, a real home they can come back to."

The words had left his mouth before he'd really thought them through.

He hadn't mentioned his marriage plan since the first night she was here, nor had she, but the more time he spent with her, the more he could see she was committed to the girls, the less claim he had on them. If she'd satisfactorily answered his question about how much she'd changed, then why couldn't he bear the thought of her leaving with them?

Because I love them.

And the ice-cold reality that he couldn't let those girls go —ever—pickaxed its way into his mind . . . and his heart.

I can't lose them.

He couldn't be denied someone he loved a second time. He'd cared for Phoebe and Zoë since the day they were born and nothing would break his bond with them, certainly not Liv taking them to the other side of the world. Maybe he really needed to consider going back to the States with them.

Something passed across her eyes as she gazed at the baby in her arms. "You mean if we were to marry, and I was to stay in Cyprus?" she said in a hesitant voice.

"Yes." He held his breath, suddenly desperate for her to stay.

"So, you're planning to live here permanently? What about your parents and your brother back in Brentwood Bay?"

"I miss my parents and my brother, of course. We all did it hard when we lost Andoni, but when I took over the business here, after my grandfather died, it gave me a new purpose in life. The business is expanding rapidly, and I have a great extended family and love being part of my Greek culture. My mom and dad visit a couple of times a year, and Alex and his fiancé Mara are coming next month."

"I don't think being split between two homes, two parents, would be as good as being with just one parent who loved them completely," she said, holding his gaze.

"People do it all the time," he said, trying to force raw

emotion from his voice. "And imagine how rich the girls' lives would be with two people who love them."

"They'll have a whole lot of people to love them in Brentwood Bay," she said softly. "All my old friends, my foster parents and my foster sister, Claudia, and her children, your mom and dad and Alex, too, if that's what they wanted. They could have the love of an extended family and people who knew their gorgeous mother. Those are the things that I longed for when I went from a family of three to just me on my own when my parents died."

"I'd move to the States if that was the best thing for the girls," he said. "No question. But that's not the issue right now. First, we must have custody assigned and then we can work out where they, and we, will live."

Her mouth formed a perfect O, and she let out an enormous yawn. "You're right, we don't need to go over this now, Markus," she said with a comforting smile. "We're both exhausted. We'll work this out in the clear light of day in the next few weeks."

He nodded. "Why don't you get some sleep?" he said, as her eyelids seemed to droop. "I think it'll be a rough night, and there's no sense in both of us being exhausted. We have to be up early to get to the doctor tomorrow, and one of us will need to be fit to drive."

"I'm fine, truly I am." She let out another yawn. "I can't imagine how hard it must've been when you were on your own with the girls, and I won't let you go through that again. We can take turns to have a sleep during the day tomorrow."

They were silent for a moment, but both babies were still grizzling.

"I've learned something since I've had the girls," Markus said, wanting to connect with her before she went to bed. He held his index finger under Zoë's hand, and she gripped it hard.

"What's that?"

"How, for the first time in my life, I'm making decisions for someone else and the pressure of that is huge."

"I know," said Liv. "I keep thinking that what we do now, the plans we make for the girls, could be very right or so very wrong."

"But we're already giving them what they need. Unconditional love," Markus said. "And if we keep that at the forefront of everything, make all our decisions with that in our hearts, we can't go wrong."

Zoë started to cry again, and he stood and moved to the kitchen. "I think I'll give her the rest of that bottle and then put her down. How's Phoebe?"

When Liv didn't answer, he pulled a warm bottle from the hot water and gave it to Zoë before snuggling her in the crook of his arm. He walked back over to Liv to find she'd dozed off, her head drooping and a ringlet across her face.

The way she sat, nurturing and protecting the child in her arms, caused a powerful bolt of understanding to singe his mind. She loved these girls as much as he did. They deserved to have her in their lives.

He thought back to his very first night in this house. The place he'd renovated after moving from Paris. Alone, and sleepless, he'd followed the path of the full moon down the cliffs to the bay, and then he'd sat on the beach, the full moon calling to him and teasing him with its rays of hope and promise.

Back then, he'd wanted to raise his head and howl for his loss; he'd been aching for the part of his heart Liv had torn away when she'd left him. Instead, he'd stripped off his clothes, given in to the moon and waded into the welcoming waters of the Mediterranean. With aching arms and bursting lungs, he'd swum out to Aphrodite's rock and then swum three times around it, all while thinking of the legend and the task he needed to complete to gain that great elusive thing—everlasting love. With Liv.

It had seemed so possible—so simple and magical—that he could make an eternal connection with the one woman he wanted more than anything else in the world. The woman who'd said it was finished, the woman who then lived thousands of miles away.

And when he'd completed the final lap, he'd stopped.

For long, long minutes, he'd trod water in a shaft of moonlight, while the tears from his eyes had mixed with the salt of the sea. And on that hot summer's night, he couldn't have imagined she'd be here one day, in this house, with two babies he'd fallen in love with. Or that he would want to do this thing together with her—be a part of the girls' lives forever—even if he could never win her heart.

Liv dreamed she was reaching out to Markus as he moved off into the distance. As she called, *I want you, I need you*, his shape grew dimmer and dimmer, his black hair whipped by a building wind as he carried the girls away in his arms.

Further and further, she stretched her arm toward him, all the while calling, *I need you, I want you*. The words that had been buried inside her so long they sounded like stone hitting glass. He couldn't hear her, he wasn't listening, and instead of bringing him closer, those words seemed to increase the distance between them.

She kept trying to touch any part of him, willing him back to her, but he floated into the distance, the girls looking up at him and smiling. And then, as she made one last, supreme effort to reach him, her arm snapped and pain screamed through her.

Something tickled under her chin, and she willed her eyes open. Her arm was pinned against her slumped body, still in the chair where she'd been holding Phoebe, but the front pack was empty and a woolen blanket lay across her torso. In a cold, sick panic, she leaped to her feet.

Where was the baby? Had she dropped her, squashed her? Shaking her head in horror as she tried to lift the fog of sleep, she picked up a cushion while her heart hammered painfully against her hollow chest. Had she left her somewhere? But as the blanket slid to the floor, reason and logic slowed her heart.

She'd fallen asleep, and Markus had taken the baby from her.

Disgust that she'd given in to her tiredness coursed through her. The bone-deep weariness was still there, but she should've resisted it, should've stayed awake to help Markus do everything with the girls as she'd said she would.

Her ears strained. Were they still awake? Had he taken them out somewhere? Silence cloaked the house and her watch flashed two thirty. It was inky dark, except where a fat slice of moon threw rays of light onto the shiny floor.

Warmth shrouded her as she thought of Markus watching her sleep and then covering her exhausted body. Even though he'd dealt with the girls on his own, he'd taken care of her, just as he'd always done in the past. An ache of tenderness stole into her heart.

Tip-toeing across the marble floor, she jumped when she stood on a squeaky toy, and her heart raced as she held her breath.

Hearing nothing, she carried on down the hallway,

breathing in the soothing smell of vanilla that grew stronger every day.

Light washed out from the open doorway of the girls' room onto the rug running the length of the hallway. She crept forward until she could peek into the room, expecting to see Markus with a baby in his arms.

Instead, the vision in front of her stole her breath and sent ribbons of love unfurling throughout her, and she fought the tears that surged from the deepest part of her.

Markus sat on the floor between the two cribs with a baby wrap draped over his shoulder and a streak of something white down the front of his shirt.

His head was thrown back, resting on the wall, and his eyes were closed, the inky frill of lashes on his cheeks a contrast to the tan of his face.

Now and then a deep breath came from between his slightly parted lips. Despite the fact he must've been exhausted, his face was relaxed—smooth except for the dark stubble across his chin.

The beauty of him asleep would've been enough to cause the rip deep within her chest, but when Liv moved closer and saw the rest of his body, she hitched a burning breath.

Each of his arms was extended through the bars of the cribs on either side of him, and the fingers on each hand were outstretched and covering the bodies of Phoebe and Zoë.

Like identical angels, the babies lay soft in sleep under the unfailing protection of this wonderful man. They were both turned toward him as if trying to get closer, their blankets tucked so carefully around their small, resting bodies. Liv could feel the love between the three of them beating and pulsing within the room.

She let her tears fall. Tears for what the girls had been through, what Markus had so selflessly done for them, and for what she—Liv—had lost with him.

How could she not have known this part of him back then? How could it be that the very parts of him she'd thought were missing—the selflessness, the responsibility, those things she thought she'd never see—be now directly in her face? Had she got it so very wrong?

Regret and confusion webbed tightly around her heart.

She reached out a hand, left it hovering just above his body, and willed the feeling of him back—for the sensations that had haunted her for the last two years to jump the void and settle softly on her skin. The warmth and strength of him, the way his muscles used to move beneath the pads of her fingers.

She closed her eyes and imagined she could touch him and be a part of him as she'd been before. If she knelt by his side, she could so easily lean forward and press a kiss to the lips she'd tasted a thousand times— the sweet taste of him part of her DNA.

Memories weren't enough, and the inches that now lay between her fingers and his body may as well have been the thousands of miles they'd been apart until now. The difference this time was that Liv could feel the possibility of that connection, the sweet threat of allowing herself to touch him, to fall into his arms again, and she wasn't sure for how long she could pretend otherwise.

But she couldn't let it happen. Not just because the stakes were so much higher now the girls were involved, but also because she couldn't hurt Markus again. He'd been hurt deeply once, and although it had been her only option at the time, she wouldn't do that to him again. By leaving him, she'd believed she was saving herself from a heartbreak she'd barely survived when her parents had been killed. She hadn't been able to face losing Markus the same way after she'd begged him to give up all the risky things that could get him killed. But she hadn't been able to face living in that constant state of fear—anticipating a phone call from an unknown number telling her he'd died —either.

This desire for him that was filling her body like a downpour on drought-stricken land had to be suppressed. He'd asked her to marry him so she could stay, so Phoebe and Zoë could have a mother. Not for any other reason.

He'd grown up, moved on—he'd even given up the thrill seeking that had been so much a part of him before. He didn't see her as a lover, or even a friend, and she had to remember that for the safety of her heart and for the girls who'd already lost one parent. If she and Markus started a relationship that disintegrated again, then the girls would lose another. She wouldn't let it happen.

She knelt down by his feet and bathed in the joy of watching him—watching him with his girls—and how it all looked so natural, so predestined. And a fresh thought unraveled before tightening around her heart. This was a bond that should never be tested, a bond that must never be undone. A father-daughter connection had been established and it mustn't be compromised.

She loved Phoebe and Zoë so deeply and could feel their personalities becoming a part of her. But how could she keep fighting to take them from Markus when the love he shared with the girls was so palpable, so beautifully in her face every day?

How could she even contemplate asking him to give these angel girls up?

7

When Liv dragged herself dripping from the shower the next morning, the shrill cries of both babies kick-started her faster than an espresso coffee. Petro's singsong voice traveled through the hall way as he tried to calm them. She wiped the water out of her eyes and reached for a robe, determined to get to the girls before Markus woke.

She hadn't woken him when the girls cried for a bottle at five thirty. He'd have been exhausted after last night, and she'd wanted to let him sleep as long as he could. He must've hauled himself off to bed at some point because the blanket she'd covered him with had been discarded in the girls' room.

When she made it into the living room with straggly hair soaking her back, Petro was holding Zoë and rocking Phoebe in the cradle swing. Both girls were wailing at the top of their lungs.

"I don't know if they need more food or to be changed," Petro said helplessly, his face drawn, eyes wide.

"It's okay, Petro." She took Zoë from him and cuddled the little girl's damp, pink cheek against her own. "I should've had my shower when they were asleep, but I thought they were settled." She threw him a wobbly smile. "Sometimes it's hard to know what they need."

"Ah, *moro mou*," he soothed as he bent down and picked up Phoebe from the swing. "I think they were looking for you or Markus."

Liv paced up and down, whispering quiet words to Zoë, but the girls crying out of control always made her tense. Sometimes they seemed to work each other up and it was so hard to get them settled. Hopefully the nightmare of last night wouldn't continue today. Her head throbbed simply imagining it.

Through her splintered thoughts she managed to remember what worked for her when she was stressed or frightened. The same thing that had set her on her path to becoming a parfumier. Breathing in a calming scent, something that reminded her of a quiet, stress-free time, slowed her heart rate and encouraged her to take deeper breaths. Maybe it would work for the girls too? She could work on some fragrances, or essential oils later, but what could she use now?

Looking around, she saw one of Markus's jackets discarded over a chair. Briefly, she remembered the orderliness of this place when she'd arrived, the austere precision of everything. Now it felt like a home, with toys in piles in the corner, shoes in a heap by the door, the scent of flowers and coffee in the air.

Something she and Markus had created.

A tremble touched her lips and tears danced across her eyes as she picked up the jacket and immediately smelled his essence—a scent that was indescribable, but a scent that was all Markus and still had the capacity to calm her. Carefully, she wrapped the jacket around the fussing Zoë's tiny body.

As if by magic, the little girl started to quieten, her grizzles turning to gurgles as a feisty little fist opened and closed on the fabric.

"That's a miracle!" Petro said, wide-eyed. "You are a genius, Liv!"

If it worked for one, would it work for two?

"Here, Petro," she called above Phoebe's wail. "Let's swap." She passed the quiet Zoë back to Petro then picked up one of Markus's shirts from a laundry basket nearby. Would it still smell of him? She laid the shirt over the wide expanse of the couch, placed Phoebe on it, and then wrapped her up. And just as miraculously, as soon as she was cocooned in the soft cotton shirt, Phoebe's cries became quiet and she turned her face as if to get closer to the fabric.

Bald reality gripped Liv's heart.

The bonding in the first few days that Markus had talked about had happened in such a basic and primal way. These girls felt safe and protected by him. It was evident right here that Phoebe and Zoë knew who had spent every day with them in the last few weeks, cared for them ... loved them.

How could she take them away from him when the deep connection they had was so obvious?

They were still and quiet, wrapped in the clothes of a man who had put everything in his life aside for them, and she couldn't take them away from that. Ever.

The same thought still swirled in her mind two hours later as she clutched a breakfast tray in one hand and knocked on Markus's bedroom door with the other.

She held her breath, imagining him tangled in sheets, hot and damp from sleep, and for a minute wondered if it would be in her equilibrium's best interest to leave the tray at the door.

"Oh, hell." His voice came through the door. "Come in."

He sat on the bed, foggy-eyed and naked from above his pajama pants, and Liv bit back a sigh of satisfaction at seeing his bare skin again. The same slim hips cut with stark muscle, the same bronzed chest she'd lain against, the muscular arms that had held her . . .

"Looks like I slept in." His mouth kicked up at one corner as he scrubbed his hands through his glossy hair. "Where are the girls?"

Liv put the tray on a side table and moved to open the shutters at the window, anything to avoid looking at him, at his muscles flexing under shimmering skin.

She bit her lip as she snuck a guilty look. "Petro and I've just fed them, and the doctor's appointment is in an hour so we're getting them dressed."

"It's ten?" he exclaimed.

She turned back and nodded, trying to keep her gaze on his face and not let it drift any lower. "You fell asleep in the girls' room last night, so I covered you with a blanket, but when I went in to feed them at five thirty you weren't there."

"Oh, yeah." He shook his head as if to banish the threads of exhaustion Liv could feel dragging in her own body. "I vaguely remember waking up on their floor with the worst pain in my back and I crawled into bed." He sucked in a breath. "God knows what time it was."

He grabbed a T-shirt from the dresser and pulled it on and her heart pulsed with the sweet, strong memory of him last night.

Two long years might have passed since she'd felt his

touch, been consumed in his kiss, but the power of him was everything she'd held in each cell of her body all that time. That memory would have to be locked down tight for all their sakes.

"How about you?" he said, letting out a low chuckle. "I'd been speaking to you for a couple of minutes and realized you'd gone to sleep."

Shocked pulsed through her. "But that's terrible! I could've hurt Phoebe."

He chuckled again and it warmed her blood. "You were holding her so close in the front pack, I literally had to prize her away from you."

"Thanks," she said, shooting him a grateful smile before looking out the window. "Have your breakfast then we can all go to the doctor's."

"Are you sure you want to come? I could just go myself." He picked up his cup of coffee and drank from it. "Thanks, for this." He grabbed a piece of toast then bit into it, tossing her a casual grin that lit up the space between them.

"Of course, I'll come, and you're welcome," she said. "We need more diapers, wipes, and formula, and it'll unsettle the girls getting in and out of the car all the time. And besides," she said, "I love being involved in every part of their day-to-day lives."

The scene of him with the girls last night, and the way Phoebe and Zoë had reacted to being snuggled into his clothes, played over and over in her mind. The nagging thought that she couldn't take Phoebe and Zoë away from here was becoming more persistent, and the most frighten- ingly simple solution just wouldn't leave her. The solution that Markus had already proposed.

Marrying him and staying here.

"I'll admit," he said, before swallowing another

mouthful of coffee, "now that I'm looking after the girls all day, not just in the mornings and evenings as I was before, I'm really feeling it. How about you?"

"Exhausted," she said, throwing him a smile. "Like my head's full of cotton wool and I've got great weights pulling on my bones. I can't help thinking how lucky we are to have Petro doing the cooking and washing, though. Imagine if it was just the two of us! Imagine what we'd be eating! Cereal for breakfast, lunch and dinner."

"It'd be hard, bringing up twins on your own."

He'd said it slowly, and Liv swung her gaze to meet his, her heart beating rapid-fire that he was reaching out to her again.

"You know the girls and I are having the paternity test done today?" he asked quietly. "I thought the sooner we get that cleared up, the better."

"Yes." She turned back to the window and the view of the dust-dry hills beyond. The confirmation would be nothing more than what she already knew—he'd told her the truth. Nobody could love the girls the way he did and deny paternity.

"I'm not sure what happened last night," she said, continuing her earlier train of thought. "The way the girls were so unsettled. I wonder if there's something we can do to help them sleep better."

"Like what?"

"Well, they didn't always seem hungry, not in the first part of the evening, anyway. They wouldn't settle until much later. One of the how-to books suggested using essential oils in the bath to calm them before they go to sleep. Something soothing that they'll associate with the routine of going to bed."

"What sort of essential oil?"

"Lavender." She turned back to him. She'd been thinking about this since she woke and she was eager to try it. "You said you have your grandfather's old still in your workshop here?" She couldn't keep the excitement out of her voice.

He stood and then pulled the snowy covers up on the king-size bed. The cotton of his pajama pants clung to long, lean thighs and she suppressed a gulp. "I'm not sure if it all works, but it's set up ready to go," he said.

"You've got some beautiful plants in front of the house and I was wondering if I could try making some oil from those."

"Have you extracted oil before?" His words trailed off and Liv basked in the warmth of his grin. "Of course, you've done it before. How could I forget," he said, the smile lingering in his voice. "It was practically all you did every weekend while you were studying."

"I haven't made perfume in a long time." She conceded. "I've been involved in the management and marketing side of the business since I've been in Switzerland, but, yes, that's exactly what I was doing in Paris."

"I think you should give it a go," he said, moving to the foot of the bed. "If anyone knows about the power of a fragrance, it's you. I don't see how it could do the girls any harm, and if it means we can have fewer nights like last night, then I'm all for it. Which reminds me," he said, "Petro planted all those vanilla orchids down the side of the house when I moved here from Paris. Part of his little plan to get me back in the swing of things. I noticed the vanilla scent yesterday and went out to have a look." His gaze skimmed her. "It's time the beans were harvested, if you're interested in helping me."

"I'd love to," Liv said, a whiz of connection rocketing through her. He wanted her here, helping him. "Now, you finish getting dressed and I'll get the girls ready."

She moved past him, but he put out a hand and touched her arm. Divine tingles rushed the length of her body as she swung her gaze to his face.

"Thank you," he said, his voice rich as velvet. "For the breakfast."

For a second she considered stepping away, but then she allowed the luxury of his warmth to peal through her. "You're welcome." Her voice was a rasping whisper. And when she looked down to where his hand sat hot on her skin, she saw her own hand covering his.

Confusion overtook her and she slowly broke the connection. "You deserved it."

Half an hour later Markus turned the car onto the main road to Paphos and accelerated. The girls were clipped into their baby seats in the back. One glance in Liv's mirror showed their faces puckered in sleep.

It took a lot to get the girls ready—making sure she and Markus had enough warm clothes, diapers, and emergency bottles prepared. She thought back to the extended lunch breaks and frequent stops for coffee during her days in the office in Switzerland; it all seemed so long ago. And she didn't miss it one bit.

She turned to Markus in the driver's seat. His hair was still damp from his quick shower. "I'll get onto the lavender as soon as we get back," she said. "Petro has said he'll help me pick some, so even though the oil will take some time to extract, I could make some lavender water for their bath tonight."

He glanced over at her and his mouth kicked up at the corners, sending a shower of sparks through her body. This was a smile all for her and she could've shouted in joy at its sincerity. "Will the house smell the way the apartment used to in Paris?" he asked. "I can still see those rose petals drying in bowls all over the living room. When I close my eyes, I can still smell the cloves and bergamot . . ." His words disappeared as he seemed to realize where he was, his face losing the faraway look of a few seconds before.

He breathed out swift words. "It was an intense time, wasn't it?" He glanced over again and this time his gaze hooked hers. "Our hunger to learn, all the new experiences, our naivete about the way the world worked."

She smiled at him. Part of her heart told her to stay away from these bittersweet memories, to keep things impersonal, but the words in her throat had a life of their own. "But we had fun, didn't we? Remember the old guy in the *boulangerie* who used to laugh at the way we pronounced *chausson aux pommes*? And the woman at the laundromat who thought we were hysterical not ironing anything?" She couldn't stop her light and breezy laugh.

The memories were so vivid, so filled with sensuality, that she could almost see the vibrant colors of market day and smell the street on a cold winter's morning. Could almost feel her hand in Markus's as they strolled by the Seine in the springtime. How he'd stopped and held her face in his hands and said, "I love you". The shiver of delight the thought of those words evoked caught her off guard.

A grin sounded in his voice when he spoke. "Remember that funny old woman who walked her dog down the street by the University? The poor little thing was dragged along as if it had never been out of its apartment and was too frightened to put one foot in front of the other."

"And she called him 'Pierre the dog' as if he might be mistaken for something else." She chuckled.

His deep, rumbling laugh erupted and blended with hers, and for one magical moment, they were joined by a gossamer strand and the magic of closeness burrowed deep in her bones.

The memory of what Markus had said about them bringing up the girls together pushed its way into her mind. They were friends. They had a shared history. They could still laugh and joke about things as they were doing now.

So why shouldn't they be able to spend their lives in the same place raising the girls? No matter how flippant Markus might've been when he first brought up marriage, it was rapidly becoming the best answer to ensure the girls' guaranteed stability. Commit to marrying Markus and stay in Cyprus. Giving the girls two parents who loved them, despite not being able to share a life together, was the only solution.

"Can you tell me why it all ended?" Markus asked in a quiet voice.

Her thoughts scrambled as she realized the conversation in the last two days had always been destined to reach this point—hurtling toward a showdown of the truth.

She slid her hands under her thighs and stared at the dappled blue sea. If there was a possibility Markus and she were going to stay in the girls' lives together—whether that was back in the States or here—they had to put this behind them once and for all. Nothing must be unspoken now, no question about why their relationship had ended unasked. They had to acknowledge what had happened in the past and move beyond it. Her heart clenched. "Are you sure you're ready to talk about this now?"

His voice was calm. "I feel as though we can talk about it, now that other things are out in the open." He pulled the car off the road. "This conversation is much too important to have while I'm driving though."

When he'd cut the engine, she counted to ten before she spoke, willing her heart rate to return to a normal level. It wouldn't.

She turned to face him and forced the words out through the staccato thump at her throat. "My leaving was bad timing. My boss was desperate to get me into the Geneva office that week. The managing director had just been charged with fraud and staff were leaving. I was in a very difficult position . . . but it was more than just work."

"You woke up one day and decided you didn't want to be with me anymore."

His flat, monotone words nicked her heart.

"I want you to know how it felt, Liv. When the bottom dropped out of my world." His gaze softened. "Now we can talk about this, I want you to know how it felt having you wake up one morning and say you had to leave. I want you to know so you never do it to the girls."

His words were shredding her.

"I had to go, Markus." Heat rose from her neck to her scalp. She'd harness some of that power and infuse her words with it. "We were finished."

The air sizzled between them.

"Were we?"

The implication that he didn't agree hung hot in the air, and the pulse beating harder in her throat prevented her from answering.

"I think you're wrong." His voice was calm and steady. "If

you hadn't been too frightened to show some commitment, I would've fought for you."

I would've fought for you.

She tried to ignore the hum those words sparked inside her. "You'd come home two days late from caving after I'd begged you not to go. You hadn't said you'd stop taking risks, so yes, we were finished." She made her words firm and confident, and he flinched.

"You weren't a risk taker when we first met. It was one of the things that drew me to you. You were so strong. So safe. And then when we moved to Paris, you changed. It was as if you couldn't live life at a fast enough speed. As if you were addicted to adrenaline, and even though that drug was coming between us, you couldn't stop."

He scrubbed a hand through his hair and blew out a breath. There was a long silence before he spoke. "It was tough for both of us moving to a foreign country. I know our parents worried about us. But when I left Mom, Dad and Alex to support Andoni, when previously we'd all done it together, it was almost as if I needed to live the biggest life I could, you know? Doing those things made my heart race, made me feel alive."

She reached out and touched his hand. When he looked up, her heart squeezed. "But you couldn't stop, even when you knew how much it terrified me."

He rolled his lips together. "No, I couldn't. I'm sorry for that now, of course. So sorry that I didn't have the strength to be open with you, to really step inside your shoes and understand what my actions were doing to you, and to us. But back then I was too . . . frightened."

"Frightened?" she whispered. When had she ever known this strong and self-assured man to be frightened?

His throat moved in a tight swallow and he rubbed his

chin with both hands. "My uncle is bipolar, like Andoni, and some people say my grandfather probably was too. I was frightened that if I didn't outrun bad feelings, if I sat and thought about things too long, it might take me over as well."

"Oh, Markus," she said, as tears pushed at the back of her nose. "I wish I'd known. Wish I could have understood what you were going through."

"And I wish I'd been open about discussing my fears with you." His face softened. "It wasn't until Andoni died that I realized how selfish my actions were. When I saw the raw and gut-wrenching grief my parents went through, I knew I never wanted to think of them going through that again. I started seeing a counselor and that's helped when things have been tough. Made me see there is help when and if I need it. I'm just glad I made the decision to change that part of my life before the girls came into it. I can't bear the thought of them losing anyone they love."

Liv pushed her palms harder into the leather seat. It was as if a light had been shone in the darkest part of her heart and a weight that had been dragging her down had finally been lifted. And a powerful thought built in her mind. Now she could fight. Now she had the sort of commitment she hadn't been able to give Markus then, and he had an understanding of what his actions had meant for her.

"I'll do it," she blurted.

She could feel his gaze burning into her as she stared out the windscreen. "I'll marry you for the sake of the girls. We'll have shared custody and bring them up together. We can live in the States, or we can live here. But I don't want a marriage just so I can get a work permit. I want to be part of their lives. Be the mother they should've had. I have what it takes, Markus."

He was silent for so long she was tempted to turn her head to see his face, but she knew that once she looked into his eyes, he'd be able to see how her announcement had scared the breath out of her. Nevertheless, she meant every word.

"Are you sure?" he finally said. "A marriage? A commitment to raise the girls? You think you can do that and not run? Keep the agreement even when the going gets tough, as it surely will?"

She flicked her hair, straightened her back, and then turned her head and locked her gaze with his. "I know in my heart that Polly would've wanted me to raise her children. But being here, I've realized how much you love them too, how settled they are and how much you have to offer them. I'm not about to rip that all away, Markus. I have the commitment. I'm doing this."

Without a word, he started the engine again and then pulled back out into the traffic, his gaze fixed on the road ahead.

"I love the girls, too, Markus. I want them to have a mother and a father in their lives and I'll do whatever it takes to achieve that."

When they pulled up outside the clinic five minutes later, Markus watched Liv unclick her seatbelt and move to open the door, but he put a hand on her arm to stop her. The girls were quiet in the back, and they still had ten minutes before they were due in the doctor's office.

The fragile warmth of her body beneath her T-shirt was achingly familiar, but he was filled with a feeling of foreboding. The shock of her announcement still reverberated through his tired body and brain.

Had she really agreed to marry him? Even though he'd wanted her to come to this conclusion, he'd never for a second imagined she'd do it so quickly.

He tried to push the image of her being with him permanently from his mind, as well as what it would do to him to see her every day—sleep tousled in the morning, curled up with a book on a winter's day, hot chocolate clinging to her lip. He had to be sure she knew what that sort of commitment meant.

He'd never told her how her leaving so suddenly had affected him, but he wanted to now so that she'd understand why he needed to believe she'd never do the same thing to Phoebe and Zoë. So that she realized what she was agreeing to.

He tried to stay calm, but his memories of that almost unbearable loss and sadness came bubbling to the surface. "How do I know, Liv?" he asked as she turned to him. "How do I know you won't agree to this and then run out when it all gets too tough?"

Her gaze was unflinching, her arm still beneath his hand. "Because I'll prove it to you."

"Can you imagine how I felt when you left me that day in Paris?" he said. "Without reason or explanation, you just said we were finished."

Her gaze softened and her eyes glistened. "I'm sorry, Markus."

He pushed on, willing her to understand the effect her decision had had on him so she'd know why she could never do this to the girls. "So why did you? I know my risk taking was a problem, and that I wasn't stopping when you asked me to was a huge factor. But we could have gone to counseling, maybe come to an understanding together about what was happening. You didn't want any of that."

He hadn't intended the words to come out in such a rush, but it was as if they'd been stoppered in a bottle and had finally found their freedom. "After everything we'd shared, the love we had, why did you walk out on all that without a fight?"

She moved her lips as if to speak but nothing came out.

"Please. I need to understand this. If we're going to make this commitment to the girls forever, I need to understand what made you run last time, so I know it won't happen again."

She closed her eyes briefly, and then she took a deep breath and pulled her arm away. "I could see my future. With all its uncertainty and tragedy, I could see a life with you panning out the same way as my past." She looked up at him, her eyes open and endless. "I asked you to stop taking risks, stop putting your life in jeopardy, but you wouldn't." She took a stuttering breath. "I imagined going to your funeral and I had to save myself from going through that all over again."

Markus rested an elbow on the door and rubbed a hand across his chin, his frustration mixing with relief that this was out in the open. "But I *needed* to do those things then." Deep inside he understood her point, particularly now he was responsible for the girls.

Liv sighed. "Markus, it doesn't get away from the fact that you lived your life in just the same way my parents did, and I couldn't put myself through the terror of a late-night phone call from an 'unknown' caller again. The fear you'd be trapped underground, or that this time your parachute wouldn't open, or any of the multitude of other things that could have gone wrong."

"But you stayed until that point. Even though you didn't want me to do those things. What made you finish everything then? Why that day?"

She sat silently, the corners of her mouth moving slightly as if she might speak, but an uncomfortable silence squeezed between them.

He turned his body toward her, cherishing the depth of their conversation and wanting to hear her say what was deepest in her heart. "You can tell me, Liv. We're miles past that point. I need to know why you left me. Why then?"

It was only one word, and she said it so quietly the inside of the car seemed to strain to hear it. "Children."

The air around collapsed in on him as his heart crashed in his chest. She'd wanted children? His baby? After he'd brought it up so many times and she'd said no? The word in all its irony cried in his ears.

He waited, his hand so close to hers, aching to reach out.

Her voice fractured. "You were late from a caving trip we'd argued over, and as I sat looking at the dinner I'd cooked go cold, I knew the waiting for you, the fear for your life, would go on forever. It had been just bearable for me, but I knew you wanted children and I didn't want any child to go through the same anguish I had. I knew where our relationship was heading, and I couldn't bring children into the world knowing they might lose a parent just as I had."

He tried to suppress it, but the sigh that squeezed from his lungs was audible. This couldn't be happening. Liv knew he'd wanted children but she didn't want to have them with him. And now that they had the possibility of bringing up children together, it was all to be part of some practical arrangement.

The cruel reality burned deep in his chest. Why hadn't he known? Why hadn't he seen it? And now she was prepared to do exactly the same thing for Phoebe and Zoë. Change her life to protect them.

The chains he'd kept wrapped around his heart for five long years burst open, and he cursed ever suggesting a marriage to trick her into showing her true colors. Now that he knew the truth, he wanted everything to be different.

8

"I'm not sure I can do this," Markus said as they sat in a sterile room at the clinic and waited for the doctor. The nurse had done the initial exam, but they needed the doctor to complete the paternity test.

"Have blood drawn?" Liv frowned. "I don't remember you being afraid of needles."

"Let the girls have blood drawn." He shifted on the hard plastic chair. "Can you imagine how they find a vein in such a tiny body?" He stroked Zoë's arm through her white cotton jumpsuit as he spoke, and his skin chilled at the thought of it.

"You'd think they'd have had blood typing done when they were born." Liv rocked Phoebe's capsule.

He turned to Liv, his unease morphing into dread. "Wouldn't you think that would be enough? Why do they have to go through this all again?"

"It's just a step in the process, Markus." She spoke quietly and he voice calmed him. "Nothing can move forward until there's proof of paternity. It's what has to be done. Surely you're not suggesting we abandon the tests altogether?"

He shook his head slowly.

"I don't want the girls to suffer any more than you do," she said, "but we need to go through this before any sort of formal custody is granted or adoption can go ahead."

He chewed his bottom lip as the doctor entered and spoke to him in Greek.

"The doctor asked if we want to do this separately," Markus explained to Liv. "Doctor, would you mind if we speak in English so Liv can understand everything?"

The doctor nodded.

"What would you like to do," Liv asked. "Would you like me to take the girls out so you can have your blood taken privately?"

"I will do the procedure on the babies first," the doctor said in English as he moved to a table covered with various vials and pieces of medical equipment.

Markus hesitated, his gaze shifting from the babies to the table and back again.

"I seem to have forgotten one of the laboratory forms," the doctor said. "I will be back in a moment."

As soon as the doctor had shut the door, Markus stood up. "I didn't realize it would feel like this." His voice was strained.

Liv's eyes widened. "What do you mean?"

"Putting the girls through this test. I'm responsible for them, and I'm making them go through pain so we can find out a fact that already exists. I'm not their father." On the last word his voice cracked, and he sat down again. "There must be another way we can work this out, some way that doesn't involve putting the girls through all this."

Liv reached out a hand to him. "We need to do this to

move forward, Markus. We won't have any claim on the girls until this step's been taken. I don't want to hurt the girls any more than you do, but we don't have a choice."

Markus picked up Zoë from her baby seat then placed his hand tenderly on her head. Warmth from her body seeped into his. Her lashes moved up and down as she blinked at him, and his throat constricted. He'd been responsible for these babies since the day their mommy died, and now he had to make decisions that could hurt them. Liv's hand was warm on his arm. Could she know the real reason he didn't want to go through with this? The devastating possibility that, when the fact the girls weren't his was out in the open, Liv would have every right to take them away? That she could leave him alone and in love with her one more time?

"We need to do this, Markus." Her words were a half whisper. "We owe it to the girls as well, to give them some sort of surety, a sense of certainty as to who they really are. We'll ask the doctor to make it as painless as possible. Maybe there's some sort of local anesthetic ointment he can use first."

The doctor entered the room again and glanced at both of them. "There is a problem?"

Markus turned to look at Zoë, so Liv answered for him. "Markus doesn't want to go through with this. He doesn't want the babies to feel any pain."

The doctor moved to the table of equipment. He picked up a long narrow cylinder, unscrewed the top and pulled out a long plastic stick with a tiny swab on the end. "We do not need to draw blood from the babies, if that is what you are concerned about," he explained. "I have blood detail taken when they were born, so in this case, I can just scrape some cells from the inside of the babies' cheeks and then place the whole thing in this sterile, sealed container to be taken to the laboratory. The babies will feel nothing more than a light brush."

Relief pulsed through Markus as he realized the girls wouldn't have to endure a needle. He sat straighter and threw a smile at Liv. It was time to move on, for the truth to be out, so they could really get on with their lives.

Emerging from the doctor's office was like stepping into a raging furnace. The sun punched onto Liv's bare skin, and she trailed a cotton scarf over her head and shoulders to try and minimize its burn.

The girls were exhausted from their wellness exam. After being prodded and poked, including having the insides of their cheeks swabbed as part of the paternity test, they were now fast asleep inside light cotton sleep sacks in their stroller.

Markus had had blood taken and had a pink and blue plaster stuck to the soft curve of his elbow.

"Too nice a day to waste." Markus grinned as he flipped sunglasses from the top of his head onto his face. "Are you hungry? I know a little *zaharoplastio* we could go to before we head back."

Liv fell into step beside him as he pushed the buggy ahead of his long stride. "A what?"

"A sugar shop." Smile lines bracketed his mouth. "They're a little like a Parisian patisserie but with lots of Greek and Middle Eastern delicacies. I think you'll like it." His delicious smile was playing havoc with her insides.

"Sounds yummy," Liv said as they made their way down the side street and joined up with a boulevard hugging the sapphire sea front. Dust from the road created a haze ahead of them and the aroma of baked earth and sea salt reached Liv's nose. It was a stunning town.

"Savvas does the best baklava I've ever tasted, and I can usually squeeze in an ice cream if I try hard enough," he said. "It's about time you started to experience some of the Cypriot culture." The warmth of his tone sang in Liv's ears. He wanted her to be here. After everything they'd said to each other, the revelations and explanations, he wanted her to be a mother to Phoebe and Zoë.

"Had you been here much before you moved to take over the business?" She looked around, taking in the gently swaying palm trees and beige buildings. "I remember you talking about traveling a bit with your parents."

"My mom grew up in a small village in the hills beyond here." He peered through the plastic window of the girls' sunshade. "I'll take you and the girls there sometime. I still have some aunts living off the land, making wine, honey, that sort of thing. You'd love it." His genuine, free smile sailed straight into her heart. "It wasn't so much of a tourist place back then, though, just a sleepy seaside town. We visited here a lot when I was little. Dad is from Lesvos, so we'd often visit there and then come here after wedding season back home. Dad's still the chef at my aunt and uncle's wedding venue in Brentwood Bay."

"Oh, that's right, I remember The Aegean Palace." She thought fondly of Markus's jolly dad, Leo, and his sweet mom, Mila. Unthinking, she touched his arm and squeezed before quickly drawing it back. "You took me there once for one of your cousin's birthdays."

"It's a pretty special place," he smiled, then looked out to the bay. "But so is this. What do you think of Cyprus, so far?"

Liv looked around her at the groups of tourists searching

through racks of swimsuits and sun hats. In the distance, people strolled along a sea wall in front of huge yachts. A couple of stocky pelicans dried their wings in the sun.

"I could get used to living here." She looked sideways at him, and his mouth kicked up at the corner. "It's gorgeous."

A barrier had lifted between them. The weight of uncertainty was gone now they'd discussed the future, and a kaleidoscope of possibilities were running through her mind. How would it work? Where would she live? They couldn't live in the same house but maybe she could rent one close by. Could she ask her boss in Switzerland about getting her old job back and working from here? She'd need to think about how she'd support herself, but it was already clear that this would be an exquisite place to bring up the girls, if that's what she and Markus both decided.

"We can go and see the catacombs some time." Markus rounded a corner, and she followed him into a little cobbled lane lined with ancient stones, worn smooth, perhaps, from lovers walking hand in hand here for centuries. "And the ancient mosaics."

Wonder bubbled inside Liv that she was sharing a part of Markus she'd never known before. Paris had been a dream, a fantasy life for both of them, and he'd spoken very seldom about his culture, and an unusual warmth enveloped her.

"Here we are." Markus stopped in front of a tiny store. A glass frontage showed a few tables and chairs scattered inside, but most of the interior was taken up by an enormous counter.

"I'm not sure if we'll fit," he said as he lined up the stroller with the doorway. The huge double stroller was never going to make it through. "I don't want to wake the girls." He tried it from a different angle.

"Don't worry," Liv said, disappointed that she couldn't get closer to the gorgeous looking cakes in the window but happy not to disturb the girls. "Maybe we can try somewhere else."

"No." Markus threw her a grin. "This is the best baklava in Cyprus. I'm not letting you miss out."

"Savva!" He called through the door, and in seconds, a huge man draped in a long white apron was chatting to him in Greek in the doorway. The rich sound of Markus's foreign words carried her away for a moment, his chocolate over gravel tone wrapping around her like scraps of silk. She'd need to learn Greek, study the culture and history, and the thought was thrilling.

"He's bringing us a table outside," Markus said. "Let's move under the shade."

Minutes later they were seated at a table, the buggy pushed in like an extra two seats. "Do we go and choose?" Liv asked.

Markus pushed his glasses up on his head and his velvet brown eyes twinkled. "I asked Savvas to bring us his finest."

One of the girls began to gurgle, and they both reached for the sunshade at the same time. Their fingers only inches apart, Liv had to ignore the bold shot of heat that burned through her as she remembered the pressure of his touch. The physical longing she had when she was near him would go away soon. When they'd worked out the practicalities of caring for the girls, those reactions would gradually diminish. She just had to ignore the intensity of them in the meantime.

She sat back, relieved to be released from the trap of her response, and she watched while Markus stood and then lifted the shade before unbuckling Phoebe and then gently drawing her from her seat. His devoted smile caused Liv's stomach to do a little flip as he raised the tiny girl to his lips and kissed her forehead.

"I'll ask Savvas to warm her a bottle." He pulled the baby bag from the bottom of the stroller. It was such a different scene from the pacing up and down in the evenings, but despite the tiredness that crawled through her veins, Markus's concern was like a thread of sunshine.

"A-ha," he said as Savvas bustled over with a tray of plates. "*Efharisto*, Savva."

The shop owner pointed to each dish and gave an explanation in Greek. There was a small plate of pastry triangles with nuts that Liv recognized as baklava, another with small pies that contained a rich-looking cream, two pots of ice cream and two of the tiniest coffees she'd ever seen.

She leaned back in the chair and sighed, letting the tension of the last few days flow out of her.

"We can order more later," Markus said, and she laughed out loud.

"This could last us for a week!"

"We'll take some *kataifi* back for Petro," said Markus as they ate. "He's got a very sweet tooth."

"Yes, let's."

"The doctor's visit went well." After testing it, Markus put the warmed bottle Savvas had delivered to Phoebe's lips. "She said paternity results will be sent out as soon as possible."

Liv twisted a serviette in her fingers. "Are you worried about what'll happen when they do come? I mean, when the authorities know you're not the girls' father, they could look for who might be."

"No one knows who he is." Markus reminded her. "Polly wouldn't tell me. She wouldn't even say what town she'd been living in. And clearly the guy didn't want anything more to do with her. He threatened her and the babies when she told him she was pregnant."

"Thank god he doesn't want anything to do with them. He sounds awful." Liv breathed relief as she cut into the triangle of baklava. "Polly was always one to give people the benefit of the doubt, so if she wouldn't say who he was or where he lived, I'm sure it was right that she kept the girls away from him." She bit into the sweet and giggled as honey dribbled down her chin.

In an instant, Markus had gathered up his serviette, leaned across the table and then gently wiped the syrup away, his gaze drilling to her core.

"No harm will ever come to Phoebe and Zoë with me around, you can count on that," he said, still holding her gaze rigid. And Liv dissolved at the intensity of his tone, the passion with which he held this one true thing so dear to him, and the way he looked at her with unadulterated honesty.

"Here, let me take Phoebe so you can have your coffee," she said, glad of the sunglasses covering her eyes so he couldn't see the effect his comments had on her.

"I'll just wind her." He carefully drew the teat from Phoebe's mouth and put her over his shoulder. His strong hand began making circles, and Liv found herself hypnotized by the way he so gently rubbed the baby's back.

"How are you feeling about what I said in the car about staying?" She spoke quietly to him while staring at his hand, her mouth dry. "Do you think we can really do this?"

She forced herself to meet his gaze, and her heart fluttered at the smile he gave her, so easy and true. He kept rubbing Phoebe's back but held her gaze solid. "I'm in this for the long haul," he said, his lips touching Phoebe's cheek as he spoke. "And I can see how much you love the girls, how much you've done already to provide them with security. If you think you can stay for the long haul too, then I'm sure we can make it work."

He saw nothing more than a practical arrangement here, and Liv had to keep reminding herself of that as he sat so close, so intensely masculine but so gentle.

She was the only one feeling the connection of old. He'd moved so far past those times that he could talk about living in the same town as her, sharing day-to-day care of the girls, without a flicker of desire.

When she could be close to him without feeling his magnetic pull, then she'd know the future was safe for all of them.

Markus finished winding Phoebe and handed her to Liv. "What will you tell your foster mom?" he asked suddenly. "You said she'd offered to help with the girls back home. Will she be disappointed that you're not coming?"

Liv's stomach contracted. "She'll be surprised," she said. "I think she thought, as I did, that this was a done deal, that you'd be glad to hand the girls over to me and that I'd be back home, so it'll be quite a shock. She's used to family arrangements changing though."

"She sounds like a lovely person."

She took the bottle and bit her lip as she gave it to Phoebe. The little girl looked at her with those huge brown eyes, and Liv's heart staggered with the love that filled her. "She's raised so many foster children," she said quietly. "I was only with her for a year but she's still happy to be a part of my life. Of all people, she'll understand how important it is that the girls are brought up in an environment of love and stability. But I would've loved for her to be part of the girls' day-to-day lives. Your parents too."

In an instant, Markus had reached a hand across the table to her. "You're giving up a lot."

She shook her head, banishing the tears that threatened to fall. "No, I'm not," she said fiercely. "I'm gaining far more than I'm giving up. Pam will understand what it feels like to be swept away by the tiniest of human beings."

Markus looked at her, his molten chocolate eyes shining. "I think what you're doing is amazing, Liv. I understand how hard it's been losing Polly, finding out about the girls and having to go through all this with me. But we can cope. We can build a life for the girls based on honesty and love."

9

Tiredness crunched Liv's bones, and although she was tempted to grab forty winks, the heat of the house in the late afternoon convinced her to harvest some lavender instead.

It had been two weeks since the doctor's visit and the deep discussion between her and Markus. They'd put their past behind them now, and it was clear they both wanted to be real parents to the girls, so it would be the best thing all round.

Wouldn't it?

Being in such physical proximity to the one man she wanted more than anything. The one man she could never have. Two sets of dark, innocent eyes stared at her in her mind and she steeled herself. Whatever feelings she did or didn't have for Markus were irrelevant. Getting in deeper with him would only cause heartache for the girls if she and Markus split up again, and she wouldn't let that happen.

And besides, Markus would never have suggested a marriage of convenience if he was still in love with her. She hadn't seen any feelings on his face or heard any in his voice. She was the only one having to rein in her emotions.

"Petro," she called. She wanted the housekeeper to help her find a basket, or at least a bucket, to collect the lavender. Her heart softened thinking of him. She'd become closer to the older man, who seemed to have taken a liking to her too.

There was no reply from the garden, the laundry room, or the other wings of the house. Perhaps he'd gone to play backgammon with his friends at the local coffee shop, which he often did after his siesta.

She went into the kitchen to clip the baby monitor to her belt and saw a letter addressed to her from her foster mom sitting in a little alcove above the counter. It wasn't unusual to receive a handwritten letter. While she regularly Face-Timed and emailed her foster mom, Pam would often send a note saying how much she missed her and how proud she was of her. Liv had enjoyed every second at Pam's house, but when Pam's husband had walked out on them, it became too difficult for the fourteen year old Liv to stay.

Apprehension prickled across her neck. Responsibility for Pam's anticipation—her joy that Liv would finally return from living overseas and bring the girls with her—seeped from the envelope to her fingers. Now she had to tell Pam she might be staying here. But she hoped that she'd understand. She'd taken in enough foster children in the past to know the impact Liv could make in Phoebe and Zoë's lives.

She tore it open and almost winced as she read it. Pam was planning to transform the whole downstairs for her and the girls just as soon as she had the word. She didn't even question what might happen if Liv didn't bring the babies home . . .

With shaking fingers, she replaced the letter in the envelope and sighed as the weight of Pam's expectations landed on her. She'd tell her as soon as she could that they hadn't decided where they'd live.

She walked the length of the hallway, wondering where she could find the tools she needed and then, against her better judgment, knocked on the door of Markus's office.

"Come in," he called from behind the heavy wooden door.

As soon as she entered the cool room, the overpowering aroma of oranges struck her. "Wow." She couldn't suppress the impact the scent had on her. It was both mouthwatering and soothing, carrying with it the memory of hot summer days as a child. "Where's that incredible smell coming from?"

Markus turned around, away from a sink; his beautiful dark eyes were framed by tortoiseshell-rimmed glasses. "It's orange essence. I'm working on a new flavor, but it's not coming together as I'd like." He took the glasses off, folded them and placed them on the counter.

"What are those?" Liv glanced at the rows of different bottles set across a long counter and moved toward them.

"New flavor blends I've been experimenting with. I'm usually not involved in this." He waved his hand across the counter. "I'm more the numbers man, but I've been disappointed with the synthetic qualities of some of the oils we've been getting, and I want to get back to basics and use some of the recipes my grandparents used. Spending the next few weeks at home while the girls get settled provides the perfect opportunity."

"Perhaps you should try making your own essences." She reached out and touched one of the bottles.

"I have been in the last few days." He grinned as he walked to a cupboard and then opened it. A little bubble of sunshine rose within her. Some of his old passion was back, his enthusiasm for tastes and smells.

"You were always the scent person. I'd like your opinion on something."

He pulled out a stack of cardboard boxes and placed them on the counter. "Have you ever tasted loukoumi—Turkish delight?"

Liv grinned. "Not the authentic stuff, I'm sure. We have chocolate-covered Turkish delight at home."

Markus slammed a hand over his heart in mock outrage. "Definitely not the authentic stuff. Our business has been around for more than a hundred years, and we've never covered it in chocolate. Take a seat." He chuckled and the bubble within her grew.

She perched on a high stool and watched, intrigued, as he removed a lid. "Now close your eyes," he said.

"Why?" Liv grinned. "Is it particularly unattractive food? Like boiled brussels sprouts or something?"

The side of his smile kicked up further. "Just close your eyes. I want you to tell me what flavors you can taste so I know whether I've got the intensity right. They're made with my new essences, and I'm hoping they'll speak for themselves." Something smoldered low in her.

He met her gaze, something sparkling in his. "Shut. Your. Eyes."

Liv grinned back and did as she was told, a small thrill working its way up her spine at the sensual image of being in this small office with Markus and boxes and boxes of sweets. And his smile . . .

"Now, open up."

The warmth of his hand came closer to her face, and despite the strong aroma of the sweet in his hand, she could smell him—the spicy, musky, sensual Markus she knew so well. She squirmed.

Then his fingers were at her lips. Fingers that knew the touch of her skin. Fingers that had traced the lines of her body were now tempting her to open her lips for him. And she did.

She sighed, not because of the velvet sweetness that melted on her tongue, but because she was so close to him again. The air around her moved and pulsed with *his* essence.

Until now, every time he'd got close it was as if she were being teased, her old longings provoked. But now a thirst was about to be quenched and she could almost feel the release.

And then his hand was gone.

But as the sweet dissolved on her tongue—the tangy bite of orange combined with the tiniest hint of mint and the rich, sweet edge of sugar—he was still there, so close that if she reached out a hand, she might touch him. Might feel his need for her without having to look in his eyes.

"Can I open?" she finally managed.

His voice was lighter. "Of course."

She opened her eyes, and he was less than a foot away, with his shoulders square and proud and his gaze burning into her own. The words he'd said in the car whispered in her ears. *I would've fought for you. I would've fought for you.* She said the first thing that came into her head. "Gorgeous."

He rolled his eyes. "What do you mean gorgeous? How's the balance of flavor, the length of taste?"

He had no idea what she was really talking about, no understanding that her words were for him. And she should keep it that way.

But all she could think about was the warmth in her stomach and the length of longing inside her.

The wish that things hadn't changed as much as they had.

"It's exquisite," she said honestly, as she crushed the desire for him that burned in every cell. "I've never tasted anything like it. It reminds me of one of the orange cordials Pam's mother made on a hot afternoon. Just oranges, oranges and more oranges."

"And . . .?" His eyes were wide, expectant. And yet the heat beneath the expectancy made her heart pound and her body clench.

"And I noticed the tiniest hint of . . . mint?" How she wished he'd keep looking at her like this forever. If only she could harness this togetherness and keep it close to her heart.

He slapped a hand on the bench making her jump. "Yes! I knew you'd pick it up. It's so subtle most people wouldn't recognize it, but it adds a layer. I knew you'd be able to sense it."

The familiarity of his comment made her want to reach out, but instead she slipped from the stool. She was filled with a sudden, desperate fear that if she stayed in here any longer, she wouldn't be responsible for her actions. She mustn't start something she couldn't finish. She'd spent the last few weeks telling him how responsible she was now, how she'd put the needs of the girls first, and that's exactly what she'd do. "It's beautiful, Markus. A winner . . ." She edged toward the door, while at the same time running her clammy palms down her shorts.

"What are you doing?" His brow lowered.

"I'm going out to collect lavender to make lavender water for the girls. They'll wake for their next feed in a little while, and I want to get this done." She tried to make her voice light. Tried but failed. The unlocked desire pounding in her veins made every word agony. Could he hear it? Feel it?

His voice was teasingly firm. "No, you don't. I have three more flavors I need you to try."

It was impossible; she couldn't go through this exquisite torture any more. "You don't need me to know how wonderful your sweets are. You said you'd lost your sense for things, but those flavors are sublime."

"I do need you," he said as he turned back to the bench and began opening another box. For a crazy minute, Liv thought he might finish the sentence the way she hoped, that after everything they'd been through, he still needed her. That he wanted her to stay here for more than just convenience, more than just to be a mother to the girls.

"My awareness of taste has improved in the last week or so and . . ." He turned around. "It feels . . . right."

His eyes sparked with veiled meaning. Whether he was speaking about the Turkish delight, or being with her, Liv didn't know; all she knew was that being here with Markus again felt dangerously good.

Deep inside, the love for him she'd kept shrouded and shut away, came struggling from its confines and sent rays of light throughout her whole body. Powerless to stop it, she let her gaze stay locked on his and savored the moment. One minute of feeding her need couldn't hurt . . .

He spoke low, teasingly. "I'm not finished with you yet. Sit down."

Dumb with want and paralyzed with possibility, Liv eased herself back onto the stool, all the while imprisoned by his stare.

"Eyes closed."

Clasping her damp palms together and willing the

tremor in her limbs to cease, she opened her mouth and felt the sweetness once more, before she again felt him step away. Opening her eyes, she found his gaze still fixed on hers, with something dark and suggestive tinting the edge of his dark cocoa irises.

"Oh," she said, among the silken sweetness. "Oh, lemon, the most beautiful lemon . . . and are the nuts . . . pistachio?"

His grin broadened, then he reached out a hand to her face. "You have sugar on your chin."

Gently, his fingers stroked her skin, and the sweetness in her mouth melded with the sweetness of his touch and she couldn't stop herself leaning into it. It might only be a hand, but the beating heat, the sure and solid strength of it, reminded her of the feel of his entire body and the promise of what he could do to her.

His finger stroked away the loose powdered sugar and then deftly moved higher up her cheek and slowly, oh so slowly, down to her neck.

Liv dropped her eyes, fearful that if she looked into his face, she might not find the emotion she wanted to see. It had been so long since he'd touched her that she couldn't tell if this was the connection of an old acquaintance or the rekindled caress of a lover.

Ignoring the rational part of herself, the part that said this shouldn't be happening, she leaned her head so the whole of her cheek was in his palm, and she absorbed the familiar connection, the wonderful feel of him, as her heart reached overdrive.

Then he stepped closer and slowly ran his finger across her lips. "And there's more sugar here," he said, his voice sexy-low. Liv couldn't stop herself from tilting her head to meet his heated gaze.

With the care of someone opening an unexpected gift,

Markus bent his head and brushed his lips across hers, at first with the slightest pause and then more firmly, definitely, as if his lips were claiming their rightful place.

In reflex, Liv parted her mouth, hungry for the intimate connection, the familiar strength and warmth, that her body knew so well. But there was so much more than she'd expected. This wasn't the kiss of familiar lovers or old and comfortable friends. This kiss held the heat of an oxygen-hungry fire, locked down too tight and for far too long.

Running his tongue along her bottom lip, Markus pulled her closer; his palms were firm on her shoulders as she leaned in and let out a moan.

Her senses were invaded in one overwhelming minute by the taste, the smell, the feel of his strong, tight body under her searching fingers. It was as if they'd never been apart, as if his essence had been so burned into her all those years ago that her deepest memory had never forgotten.

The kiss deepened and Liv's head spun as something worked its way around her throat. The tight squeeze of sadness that she'd had to give all this up became more and more pronounced as she found herself falling deep into Markus once more.

"Liv, Liv." He pulled away to breathe then trailed kisses down her cheek to the hollow of her neck.

The sweet, heavy tightness in her throat blocked all words as she held him closer. The ecstasy of his breath against her skin was overpowering, and she willed this moment to last forever, knowing the second they pulled away they'd have to realize this was a terrible mistake.

She pulled his head down to her shoulder so she wouldn't see that same knowledge in his eyes. No matter how much her heart had leaped when she'd heard him say he would've fought for her, she couldn't get away from the fact that it wasn't just about them anymore.

Squeezing her eyes tight, Liv remembered the pledge she'd made to herself. To marry him for the sake of the girls. For no other reason. That's all he really wanted.

So, was he only doing this so she'd stay and not leave him like she had before?

Markus closed his eyes for a second. The feel of her, the taste, was just as all his dreams had promised, and although he'd warned himself away from this, nothing had ever felt so right. If he kissed her long and slow one more time, it might be as though they'd never been apart. That in doing so he wasn't opening himself up to be let down again.

Mentally stamping down sense and reason, his body called for more of her, and he lifted her T-shirt and ran his fingers across her velvety waist. He wanted to know this woman, to understand how he hadn't seen the real Liv before, the person who had such a capacity for love that she'd put the needs of others first.

Her trembling hand covered his, and he opened his eyes as she murmured his name and the need pounding through his blood grew.

"Markus . . ." Her voice, a shy whisper, broke through his tumbling mind.

Her hand removed his, and she was pulling back and lifting her chin until their gazes met in hot pause.

"No, Markus," she said with soft certainty.

She let his hand drop then and slid from the stool, away from the small circle of pleasure that had so briefly held him. "This is not what either of us truly wants . . . or needs."

He didn't speak. This was *exactly* what they both wanted and needed. He knew the responses of her body intimately, and despite his surprise that it was still there, she couldn't hide her desire for him, he'd felt it pulsing through his fingers.

He waited for the words to leave her lips. The same words she'd said the last time she'd pulled away from him like this.

"It's understandable we should feel emotional, especially . . . after what . . . we've been through in the last few weeks, but . . ."

Each word came out in a breathless rush, belying her façade of control. "This is the sort of thing that would . . . make a marriage for the girls' sakes impossible."

Still, he didn't speak, just watched the ragged words trip out of the mouth he wanted to devour more of.

Her face was pained with raw uncertainty. "I think we can acknowledge," she said, her voice shaking as she took another half step back, "that we're both looking for some closure here and—"

"Are we?"

She was lying, fooling herself. She might try to make her words formal and distant but their real meaning was desperately obvious in the heat radiating from her and the indecision swimming in her eyes.

"We'll get married for one reason only, so the girls can have two parents." She placed her palms on her cheeks and blew out a sharp breath. "We both know that if this tragedy hadn't occurred, we wouldn't be in this room right now. We'd be miles away from each other, because that is the best thing for us."

She stopped speaking as if waiting for him to respond, but he kept his words confined, hot in his throat. He couldn't believe she was saying this, not after the fire he'd felt in her touch and the need he'd recognized in her body. In one kiss, she'd confirmed her desire for him was still alive.

She blinked quickly then continued. "So, we have to do what we've both pledged and put Phoebe and Zoë first."

The unexpectedness of her resolve and the deep meaning in her words held him silent. Loving was hard for her, something she'd had to learn after what had happened to her parents. And learning the importance of commitment was part of that. That he hadn't seen it when they'd been together before was a tragedy; that she was now saying having it for the girls would keep her from him was unthinkable.

And it made his desire for her burn hotter than he'd ever experienced.

"I'm not looking for any closure, Liv." He had to be honest, but the effort of dampening his feelings to hold a rational conversation wasn't easy. "I'm just interested in the here and now." He kept his voice low, willing her to step closer once again. He wanted to stop talking, stop rationalizing and reasoning, and just forget all this in a kiss. But he knew she'd meant what she'd said.

Her voice dropped a little and he could sense something like regret in her tone. "But the here and now isn't what counts, Markus. It's the future. Phoebe and Zoë's future. And you and I need to put aside in-the-moment desires for something far greater. Phoebe and Zoë's happiness." Her voice shook. "I don't want to hurt you again, but I won't hurt the girls. And that's what would happen if you and I fell into a relationship again. It would end the way it did last time, with acrimony and bitterness."

He took a deep breath to aid the journey of his words. "Of course, you don't want to hurt me, Liv, and neither do I want to hurt you, but if we're going to bring up the girls together, we can't deny the attraction between us."

This time her words were stronger. "We *have* to deny it, Markus. We have to fight for what's best for the girls."

"And what would happen if you and I had something worth fighting for?" He leaned back against the bench to stop himself from reaching out and holding her so she could feel the truth of his words, feel the desire in his fingers when he touched her. "If the feelings we've both experienced in the last few minutes are real? What if we decided we want to be together? Really together, working on our relationship, creating a family with the girls, loving each other and loving them. Why would that be so terrible?" He held his breath for an agonizing moment as he watched her face tighten.

She touched both hands to her delicate cheeks and closed her eyes as if the thought horrified her. "Because they've already lost one parent. Imagine if you and I were to try and patch things up, stitch our broken love for each other back together. Then when it didn't work out, they'd be devastated. We'd all be devastated. And potentially split between two distant countries. I haven't committed to marrying you to have it all become impossible because we let desire get in the way. We did that once before and it ended in heartbreak."

She opened her eyes and turned her head to look at a spot on the wall. "And if we made each other crazy enough back then . . ." She paused, then turned to really look at him. When she spoke, her voice had softened. "Oh, Markus, don't you see how awful it would be if we dragged children into it? If we hurt those beautiful girls because we failed as we did before?"

He held his gaze on her face, willing her to really see at

him so she'd know he meant this. "People change, Liv. Look at me. I'm not the high-flying litigator I always dreamed I'd be. I'm in my mom's home town running a confectionery business." He ran his hands through his hair. "We were young then, Liv, full of ourselves and the possibilities life held for us. And we were in love."

He took a step toward her. "Now that we're older and wiser, we can make things work this time. You just need to stop denying your feelings. I can see it in your eyes. Have faith in us."

Her shoulders tensed and then she pulled away. "Phoebe and Zoë is what I need to put my faith in right now. Not the fragile thing that was our old relationship. We can have a *new* relationship now, Markus, one based on friendship and a mutual love of the girls." Tears shone in her eyes, her voice flat and defeated as she crossed her arms in front of her rigid body.

"We can be together, Liv. If you want it enough. Let go of the past and listen to your feelings."

Her eyes snapped back to his, but he continued. "What you say about protecting Phoebe and Zoë from losing another parent is true. But the greatest gift we could give those two girls is parents who love each other as much as we love them. And it's something we can fight for. Until today, I had no hint that you still had any desire for me. But now, after that kiss, after the way I felt you respond in my arms, I don't doubt it. And I'm certain of the way I feel about you."

Her intake of breath was so sharp it cut the air. "Markus—"

He held up a hand. "I understand how much I hurt you before, and I'm so deeply sorry for that. I regret not telling you my biggest fears, and I know that's a big part of why you had to leave. I know now that you can be committed, that you can show the deepest love, and when you come to understand that you do have the commitment and love for me that I know is there . . ." He paused, then pinned her with his stare. "I'll be waiting."

Her throat moved in a tight swallow before she spoke, and he knew that his words had touched her deeply. But she held her chin higher. "Markus . . ." Her voice dropped. "It's lovely . . ." She took another breath. "What you said."

She stopped and cleared her throat, then pulled herself taller and her gaze sharpened. "But you're only saying these things because you're frightened I'll take the girls away, that I'll leave you the way I did before. But I won't. I've made the decision to stay and be Phoebe and Zoë's mother, with you as their father. You don't have to . . . touch me or kiss me to get me to do that. What we might have wanted once is irrelevant . . . no, *impossible* now that we have Phoebe and Zoë to care for. We can't risk their lives, their stability, because of desires that in the end cause us to hurt each other. I won't let it happen."

A whimper from the monitor indicated one of the girls was stirring, and she stepped back and looked at her watch. "I need to get the girls' bottles ready."

As she looked up, he held her gaze rigid. "You're wrong." Things had changed now, and she didn't have to pretend anymore. He knew she felt as strongly about him as he did about her.

"This can't happen again, Markus," she said, her voice cool and fluting as she moved toward the door. "And there's no point in you waiting for anything. The only reason I'll marry you is to provide a happy and secure life for Phoebe and Zoë and nothing will jeopardize that."

10

"*L*iv, Liv, are you there?" Petro's voice was high with anxiety the next morning.

Liv wiped lavender petals from her hands on a stiff white apron and hurried to open the door of the shed.

"What is it, Petro?" Her heart raced at the look of terror on his pale face. "Is it one of the girls? What's happened?" Her stomach pitched and rolled. She'd die if anything happened to them.

"It's the social worker," he said in his thick accent. "She is here, one hour early, and I have not even finished frosting the cakes!"

The tight coils of dread within her began to unwind, and Liv grinned as she patted his tense shoulder while they walked inside. Markus was talking to Ana-Maria in the living room, and Liv began moving to join them, cringing at the piles of washing that hadn't been put away, as well as the wraps, the play gym, the music box. Why had Ana-Maria come so early? To see how badly she and Markus kept house?

Petro forced a whisper. "I'm sorry, Liv. I should have

tidied up, but I was putting a mobile up above the girls' cribs and then I got carried away with the cakes and—"

Her stomach clenched tight again, but she patted Petro's arm. They were all doing their best to care for the girls, but would Ana-Maria see it that way?

She wiped her hands across her skirt, at the same time trying to smooth down her fears. What Markus had said last night about waiting until she came to him had rocked her to her core. It mustn't happen again—him getting so close that her resolve and her body melted. She had to remember he was only reacting like this to keep her here.

The kiss they'd shared had been magical and his touch had been the realization of a bottled-up fantasy, but she knew his reaction to her was based on his fears that she would leave again, nothing more.

Even if only a fraction of his reaction was genuine, the fact was they'd tried and failed once before to make a relationship work, and this time four hearts could be broken. Above everything, he would never trust her. He'd always be waiting for the moment she took fright and ran because of something that might happen between them, and she couldn't let that uncertainty and mistrust taint Phoebe and Zoë's lives.

Now that she'd made the decision to stay here, she wouldn't let such a fragile arrangement be destroyed for a moment of pleasure. No, she had to keep her physical distance from Markus and make him see that she could rise above her need for him. When he realized he didn't need to say these things to make her stay, she was sure they could get on with the business of being parents and, just as importantly, friends.

"I'm sorry to arrive before our scheduled appointment time," Ana-Maria said, as Liv joined her and Markus. The other woman reached out and shook Liv's hand. "I explained to Petro and Mr. Panos . . . to Markus that I've been unexpectedly called to a court case this afternoon and this is the only free time I have for the next couple of weeks. I hope you don't mind, but I didn't want to keep you waiting that long."

"No, not at all." Liv pushed a washing basket out of the way then moved to sit down. Petro had become as enthralled with the girls as she and Markus were; all three of them would rather be with Phoebe and Zoë than tidy up. She tried to gloss over the mess. "I should've cleaned this up sooner, but I got a little carried away with making a sleeping balm for the babies."

Ana-Maria shot her a quizzical look. "There's nothing wrong with having baby things around." She moved a teddy bear from beneath a cushion and sat him up beside her.

"I will make coffee," Petro said, before nodding his head and leaving them.

"The babies are asleep, I assume." Ana-Maria smiled first at Liv, then Markus.

"Yes."

"Yes."

They spoke simultaneously, and when she turned to him, Liv could see reassurance in Markus's endless coffee-colored eyes. What he'd said to her last night kept playing over in her head.

I'll be waiting for you.

Why did he believe she would come back to him? Had she given him false hope? Been too open?

Ana-Maria was talking to Markus, and Liv turned her attention back to what they needed to do this morning.

They'd agreed not to tell her of their plans to marry just yet. If they did well enough in today's interview, Ana-Maria might not suggest foster care again. They needed the authorities to see that the girls were in the best possible hands.

"They're due to wake in about half an hour." Liv glanced at her watch before folding one of the girls' wraps into a tiny square.

Markus nodded in agreement. "They've been down for about two hours, haven't they, Liv?"

The social worker closed the file she was holding and placed her hands on top of it. "Good. That's enough time for me to speak to the two of you together then." She looked at them in turn as she spoke. "You seem less . . . antagonistic than the last time I saw you." A friendly smile touched her lips.

"We've managed to work some things out." Markus's voice was sexy-low, and suddenly Liv could feel his lips still branded on hers and the hum that still resounded in her body from his touch yesterday.

Ana-Maria looked intently at Liv. "So, you think you work well as a team in the care of the children?"

Liv shifted in her chair, surprised that Ana-Maria was asking about how they parented together. She'd been under the impression this interview was about which of them would be best suited for long-term custody.

"We're managing really well," she said quickly, happy to be honest and proud of what they'd achieved so far.

Ana-Maria continued. "And what do you see as Mr. Panos's strengths when it comes to caring for the girls?"

Time seemed to stop, and Liv could feel the eyes of both Ana-Maria and Markus on her. She hadn't said enough of this to Markus yet, how incredible he was with the girls, how much love he had for them, but the honesty in her answer made the words come easily.

She squeezed her hands together then turned to Markus as she spoke. "He gives the girls his time. He's patient with them." The more she said, the more she couldn't drag her eyes away, and the words tumbled out. "He's committed to their routine but doesn't get upset if things get a little out of kilter. And," she turned back to the other woman, her heart thumping, "he's put his whole life on hold for them."

Her heart cracked and a hot breath caught in her chest. She looked down, afraid to look at him, afraid he'd see the raw emotion on her face. She fought to gain control.

Confusion sat on top of the tangle that lay deep in her core. Why was it that one moment she had everything sorted, everything rationalized, and then one look, one word from Markus, could cause her body to hum and her mind to race again?

Ana-Maria turned to Markus. "And what do you see are Ms. Bailey's strengths, Mr. Panos?"

Holding her breath, she looked up. The power of his gaze heated her cheeks, and her heart doubled its pace as she fidgeted in her chair. "Her newfound ability to fight so strongly for something she believes in," he said, his voice strong and true.

Her insides crumbled.

Her ability to fight for something she believes in.

The thing she'd known he was testing her on from the moment she'd arrived was no longer an issue. He really believed she'd changed. Liv saw Ana-Maria's mouth moving, but her ears were deaf to what the other woman said.

The only thing her mind could register was the stark reality that had struck her. He recognized she could fight and knew she was capable of seeing things through. A glow began inside her. Markus, the one person who knew her better than anyone, had recognized what she'd done.

She rolled her bottom lip through her teeth.

"Excuse me, Liv?" Petro's voice broke through her galloping thoughts. He held up her phone. "Your phone has rung a few times. The screen says it's Pam. Would you like me to call back and say you're busy? I was worried it might be important."

Liv looked first at Markus, then Ana-Maria, and cleared her throat. Her daydream had shattered, bringing her back to reality with a thud. "I can call her back later."

"No," Ana-Maria said. "You take the call and I'll have a chat with Markus about a few things. Then when we're finished, I can talk to you alone."

Perhaps it was better if she left now, to save any more revelations.

"I'll be on the deck if you need me." She took her phone from Petro and made her way outside.

She sank back into the outdoor couch so she could see Markus and Ana-Maria inside, then she took a deep breath and tapped the redial button. She put the phone to her ear. "Pam?"

Her foster mother spoke in an excited rush. "Livvy, it's so good to hear you. We haven't spoken since you got to the house. How are the girls? I bet they're growing fast. How's everything going? Are you managing in that awful situation?"

This wonderful woman—who'd opened her heart to Liv, and before her many other foster children—could always sense the truth, so there was no point telling her anything else. However, she still didn't know Markus wasn't the girls' father, so Liv would try to avoid that topic—as Markus had asked her to—until it was all official. "It's not awful, Pam, it truly isn't." Liv let her gaze drift inside.

Markus's hands moved through the air as he spoke to

Ana-Maria about the girls. Anyone could see how much he loved them. "Markus has been wonderful with the girls, and he's accepted me being here much better than I could've imagined. It's very hard on him, you know," she said in a soft voice, swallowing over the lump in her throat.

Pam wasn't one to judge others, and her response was just as diplomatic as Liv would've expected. "It's a very difficult adjustment for you, too, sweetie."

"But he's put his whole life on hold for them. He loves them as much as I do."

"There can never be too many people to love a child, Liv, so if he does that's a wonderful gift."

Liv couldn't speak and Pam spoke again, her voice carrying a forced breeziness. "I'll begin the renovations as soon as you get the go-ahead from the court, dear. I'll be completely ready when you bring the girls back to Brentwood Bay, so you have nothing to worry about. Everything will work out just fine."

"Pam . . ." She couldn't drop the bombshell just yet, but she needed to sow the seed that she might not be coming back with the babies. "You know there's a chance that Markus will keep the girls here." She bit down on her lip.

"Of course, dear. I know that, but I'm staying positive, and I hope you are too."

"Yes."

Ana-Maria's laugh from inside reminded Liv that she'd be interviewed on her own soon, and the thought of being able to talk about Markus and the girls made her heart lighter.

Her foster mother's voice broke into her thoughts. "We just need to think of what Polly would've wanted, Liv. That's all that matters."

"Yes, you're right." Liv continued to watch Markus and

her heart began to thud. She couldn't deny it anymore—the fantasies that were born whenever he looked at her a certain way or used a certain tone, or when he'd kissed her so passionately in his office yesterday. Or when he'd told her he'd wait for her. She had to stop herself getting close to him before everything unraveled. Now that she'd decided to marry him, more than ever she needed to convince him they could never be together.

The stakes—the stability and happiness of two beautiful little girls—were much too high.

"Custard pie?"

"Pardon?"

Petro handed Ana-Maria an enormous plate of cakes and slices. Markus had just left them so she could interview his housekeeper. "I also have some *tiropites* in the oven." He smiled at her, the tan of his face contrasting with his salt and pepper hair. "Cheese pies."

He was exactly the opposite of what she'd expected from their brief chat on the phone. She'd imagined some white-haired grandfather in his seventies with flour under his fingernails, but the man sitting in front of her looked like someone out of a forties movie. He wore a jacket and tie, his hair was cut short, and he had midnight eyes that twinkled. He could be early fifties—no, the lines on his face were character filled, not from aging—maybe late forties?

"Are you foreign?" he asked, and she suppressed a smile at the well-known Cypriot skill of getting straight to the point.

"I'm from Canada." She picked up the tiny cup of coffee

and delicate serviette he'd put in front of her. He rubbed his hands across his thighs and shot her a nervous smile.

She shifted in her seat. "I was born here but left when I was eighteen. I came back two years ago when my mother was ill and just stayed. I was the only one of my siblings who wasn't married and—" She took a quick sip of coffee and the hot liquid burned her lip. The only unmarried sibling! What was she thinking! She was supposed to be interviewing him about Markus and Liv and the babies, not blabbering about herself.

Petro cleared his throat as a tiny grin danced on his lips, and he offered her a second plate of sweets. "You might like the chocolate things there," he said, pointing. "Apparently they're well known in America. I made them for Liv."

She took the delicious looking square.

"How long have you been Markus's housekeeper?"

"Two years. It began as a favor while he re-established himself back in Cyprus, and like you, somehow I've never left."

"Mmmm, these brownies are gorgeous." Crumbs tumbled down her chin.

"I'd worked for Markus's grandfather for many years, and while I didn't know Markus well before he moved here, he made me an offer I couldn't refuse."

"*I'd* pay you to make food like this for me. My mother says her greatest failing was having a daughter who cooked like a prison warden."

Petro let out a hearty chuckle. "All you need is someone to teach you. Someone who'll take the time to show you the beauty of food and how to prepare it simply."

"I'd love to have someone teach me."

The tan on his face deepened. "The *tiropites*!" he said, and then rushed into the kitchen.

Murmurings from the baby monitor indicated the twins were stirring, and first Liv and then Markus could be heard talking to them. Ana-Maria leaned over and switched the machine off.

"So, tell me," she said, moving to a stool by the kitchen counter. "How do you think Markus and Liv are coping with looking after the twins. It's a big job for people who've never had children."

Petro took off his jacket and rolled up his sleeves, and she wondered if he'd got dressed up for her benefit. He looked more relaxed as he opened the oven door to remove the pastries.

"I won't pretend it hasn't been stressful," he said. "When it was just me and Markus it was busy enough, but since the girls became more wakeful, it's been very good to have three of us taking care of them."

She leaned her arms on the counter. "Does that mean you think it would be too difficult for Markus to look after the babies if he only had you to help out?"

He placed the hot tray on the counter and the smell of savory cheese and herbs surrounded them.

"I think it's always difficult to look after babies, but if you love them enough, then you just cope no matter how many of you there are. That's what I did when I brought up my own children after my wife died young. They weren't babies, but they were still quite small."

"That must have been very difficult." His face softened and her chest pulled tight. "How old are your children now?"

"All in their twenties and happy enough in their lives, which is all a father can ask. I missed their baby days though, so it's been a privilege to help with Phoebe and Zoë."

His hands moved quickly as he glazed the tiny triangular pies and dusted sesame seeds over the top. Privileged. Such a lovely word for him to have used.

Ana-Maria sat straighter on the stool. "So, in your opinion, how well are Liv and Markus working together in their care of the babies?"

He shrugged. "It would be fine if they didn't make each other crazy."

"They fight?" she said, making a mental note.

"No." He pulled a plate from a cupboard and started piling it with the pies. "They love each other."

"They what?"

Petro stopped what he was doing, and his mouth quirked in a warm smile. "Haven't you noticed the way his eyes follow her when she moves?"

"Not really."

"Or the way she touches her lips when she's speaking to him?"

Ana-Maria eased her collar away from her neck. She'd never known a man to be so observant of people's actions and emotions. "No, I haven't."

"Cheese pie?"

Although she was stuffed from the brownie, she couldn't help but reach for one of the savories.

"A man can't think straight when he's in love with a woman. Can't focus on his work, his house. Anything. When a man's *crazy* in love with a woman, he's about as helpless as a baby himself."

Was he being serious? And then she saw the crescent of dimple that bracketed his mouth.

"And women don't do that?" She should keep this conversation professional, but there was something in his teasing tone that she wanted to hang onto.

"Women are good at distractions." He put a plate in front of her, put three more pies on it and leaned his elbow on the counter. "They get things done, become super-efficient beings, whereas men can only focus on one thing at a time." His gaze held hers, and for the first time in ages, Ana-Maria's heart swooped.

"You sound as though you've had a lot of experience."

"Not enough," he said, and a flutter danced in her throat before she cleared it away.

"So, tell me more about how you think Liv and Markus are going to work things out."

"I'll help you clean up." Liv smiled at Petro as he scrubbed the countertop, a towel flung over his shoulder.

He'd produced cakes and pies and tiny sweets on spoons for Ana-Maria, and as the lazy warmth of the afternoon filtered through the house, Liv breathed a sigh of relief that everything had gone so well.

"Thank you for what you did today," she said as she picked up a tray and began to wipe it. "I can't believe all this food you made for Ana-Maria. I thought you were going to ask her to stay for dinner you kept talking to her for so long."

A tinge of red crept across his cheeks and he turned away from her. "You're welcome," he said gruffly. "She was interested in the girls, that was all."

Liv suppressed a grin. "I don't think Phoebe and Zoë were the only thing she was interested in."

He made a blustering sound, and she decided not to keep teasing him. "Thank you, Petro."

He turned around. "What for?"

"You've been so wonderful with the girls, and I know you didn't find it easy having me here in the beginning."

"I thought you were a very strange, nanny," he said, laughter in his voice. "I'd never seen someone struggle to put a diaper on the way you did."

Liv shot him a grin. "I was pretty hopeless that first night, wasn't I?"

"You wanted to do everything on your own, and it's not possible with two babies," he said. "You know how to share things with other people now."

Liv wondered if he meant more than just the care of the babies, but she brushed the thought aside. "I think we managed to convince Ana-Maria today that the girls are being well cared for."

He looked at her from under his bushy brows, charcoal eyes twinkling. "We made a good impression, I think. She will see that you and Markus will make the best parents for Phoebe and Zoë."

Liv's heart began to race, and the tray clanged against the marble countertop in her unsteady hands. "What do you mean?"

Petro knew nothing of their marriage plans, only that Markus was applying for custody and Liv was helping him out.

He carried on cleaning but let out a low chuckle. "You think I don't see what's under my very nose."

Heat rose rapidly on her cheeks. She turned away and then pretended to search for a place to store the tray. "Markus and I are working together to make sure Phoebe and Zoë are happy," she said swiftly.

"This house hasn't known such love in a long time," he said matter-of-factly. "In the time I've been coming here since Markus moved in, it's been cold and empty, but not anymore. Anyone with eyes in his head can feel the love swimming in this house."

"We certainly all love the girls." She put the lid on a cake tin and moved toward the pantry. He knew more than he was letting on, and it made her squirm.

"I'm not speaking about the girls," Petro said in his rich accent.

He stopped speaking, so Liv turned around to face him. Words wouldn't come as his gaze hooked hers. "It is very important to me that Markus isn't hurt, Liv. I've watched him pick himself back up in the last two years, and I don't want him to go through all that again. He's come too far."

His tone was soft and fatherly, but Liv could hear the warning in his voice. "When he returned from living in France, he was a broken man. It took us a long time to convince him to forget you and move on with his life, and it's been a slow process. He never mentioned your name, so I didn't make the connection when you first came here. He's used this house as a refuge to heal in, as a place to find his old self. Now that you are back in his life, I fear that he might lose himself again."

"I don't want anyone to be hurt, Petro."

He reached out and touched her arm, and his gaze was soft but holding her still. "I'm sure that wouldn't be your intention, my dear, but anyone can see that Markus cares deeply for you. He's never put away the love he had for you, and I see it growing every day. I'm not sure you feel the same way, and I don't want him to go through losing you again or those precious girls."

Hot tentacles wrapped around her chest and she struggled to take a breath. She'd grown to care for Petro, and she knew his appeal to her was based on his respect and love for Markus, rather than a desire to upset her. As he held her gaze, she couldn't help feeling he knew the secrets locked down in her heart, and it made her sick to her stomach.

"Things are difficult, Petro," she said on a breath.

"Love is *always* difficult, Liv. The trick is to never forget that and never take it for granted that things will be easy."

"I wouldn't, I don't . . ." The darkest worries that had been buried inside her were now exposed in Petro's words. Agreeing to marry Markus had never been a simple solution, but now she wondered what she'd been thinking. It was cruel to give him hope and make him relive their past all the time. She couldn't hurt him all over again. Couldn't let herself be hurt. She had to pull back and find some sort of distance before they crossed the line.

Petro turned away from her and began to speak about what he'd prepare for dinner, but she only heard half his words as her mind began to race.

Liv watched Markus pour some of the lavender water she'd made that afternoon into the baby bath and swirl it around with his fingers. The real oil wouldn't be ready for some time, but this might work just as well. They'd been up most of last night again, trying to settle Phoebe and Zoë.

She'd washed the sheets from the girls' cribs in the lavender water today, and their whole room smelled like a field full of wildflowers.

"Stop wriggling, you." She smiled down at Zoë in her arms. The tiny girl's head turned and her whole face broke out in a wide-mouthed smile.

And Liv's heart burst.

"Oh, Markus," she said, her voice wobbling with wonder. "Come quick! Zoë smiled!"

"Come on, sweetie," she said to Zoë. "Do it again."

"Hey, Zoë," he said from behind Liv. The heat of his closeness began seeping its way through her rigid body.

He'd been cool with her since their time in the office. They'd made it through each part of the girls' routine without referring to their discussion. It was no wonder he was a little distant—given the way Liv had dampened down his attempt to get closer—but she needed to make it clear that no amount of waiting for her would weaken her resolve that they couldn't be together.

He spoke gently and lovingly to Zoë. "Give me a smile, come on, honey."

And Zoë turned to where he stood, and her face broke into another heart-melting smile.

Liv couldn't help herself, she had to see his reaction, and when she looked into his face, his response was powerful enough, potent enough, for her to swallow back tears of pride and wonder. It was the sort of expression he used to have when he looked at her—overwhelming, all encompassing. The way his eyes creased at the corners and lit up when he looked at the gorgeous little baby in front of him made Liv want to make this feeling happen over and over again. She wanted him to experience that feeling every day of his life.

"Would you look at that beautiful girl," he said softly, as he moved and brushed Liv's shoulder. "You know, I think she recognizes my voice now."

A lump set solid in her throat, and Liv could say nothing, could squeeze no sound past it. While she stroked Zoë's arm and her heart swelled with love for this tiny being, she realized she'd fallen head over heels for this little girl and her sister and this snug little unit the four of them had created.

"Should I take her to the bath?" Markus tickled Zoë's belly.

"No, I'll do it," she said, then searched for a reason for them to be in the room together. "Could you get Phoebe ready?"

It was quiet for a few moments, as Markus whispered to Phoebe while she kicked in her crib, and Liv set about washing Phoebe's sister.

"How did your time with Ana-Maria end up?" Markus asked, as Liv shampooed Zoë's dark hair with care, remembering how nervous she'd been the first time she'd held this tiny human in her arms. It now felt so natural.

"To be honest?" She smiled down at the wriggling baby and started to wash the body that was filling out by the day. "It was great to be able to tell her how we've been managing, how we've worked together. But mostly I felt proud telling her how supportive you've been and how wonderfully selfless you've been the whole time I've been here."

He picked up Phoebe, who'd begun to fuss, and held her in the crook of his arm. Strength and tenderness rolled into one.

He came and stood beside her. "Thank you."

For a long moment, she considered changing the subject or laughing off his response. But she couldn't; they'd come past that. She swallowed. "You deserve it. And I'm only glad we've decided I'll stay, because I certainly couldn't imagine making up stories about you if I was trying to get custody."

His gaze scanned her and his voice lowered to a sensual almost-whisper. "I felt the same way. I told her what a wonderful mother you are for the girls."

She suppressed a gasp, and then she spoke quickly so he wouldn't notice the effect his words had on her. "Thank you." Her whole body warmed as she thought about him saying those things to the social worker.

"It's true. I can't believe the changes I've seen in you since you've been here—the way you've put the girls first, the way you've decided to fight for them. I've seen a completely different side of you. A side I never thought I'd get to see."

Liv tried to make her voice calm over the emotion that raged through her. "That's a lovely thing to say."

His voice stayed soft. "I meant it."

Her breath hitched. "I know."

"And not because I wanted her to see us as a couple."

She focused her gaze on Zoë. "Markus, we're not a couple and we're never going to be."

"But immigration can't know that. If we decide we're staying here."

His tone cushioned her disappointment as she soaped Zoë.

She had an overwhelming desire to keep this connection with Markus, but the more they talked, the more confusing everything became. He needed to understand her completely on this. "I know, but they're the only people who'll see our marriage as real."

To her surprise, Markus let out a low chuckle. "Petro told Ana-Maria he thought you and I were the perfect people to bring up the girls."

Liv swung her gaze to his as a pulsing warmth radiated through her. "He told Ana-Maria that?"

Markus's grin was broad. "That's what she told me. He's become very fond of you, you know."

He moved to the head of the bath and she could feel him watching her. "I'd like your opinion on something."

Liv lifted Zoë out of the bath and then transferred her to

the big white towel waiting on the change table. "My opinion?"

Zoë was quiet while Liv rubbed her dry, but Phoebe was fretting. "What about?"

Markus paused for a moment then spoke with assurance as he moved to Phoebe. "I wonder if it'd be right to have the girls christened."

Phoebe's wail drowned the half-cry that left Liv's lips. Feathers of love for this wonderful man, for the way he felt about these babies, wrapped around her heart again. She used every ounce of effort to calm her words. "Christened?"

He held Phoebe over his shoulder and began rubbing her back, and his voice was quiet, but commanding, as if he'd put a lot of thought into this. "It's something that happens to most Greek Orthodox children at this age, and I thought it'd be a good way to honor where they were born. It would need to happen soon, and if Ana-Maria didn't object, I'd like to make the arrangements. It could be the first official thing you and I do together for the girls."

Pride swelled inside Liv. He was thinking about the girls' future, about values and beliefs and the way he'd like to bring them up, and it made her weak with wonder at his thoughtfulness.

'We could meet with our local priest next week to discuss it at least." He looked at her with softness. "We could go together."

Liv swallowed. She'd never been much of a churchgoer, but this wasn't about her. This was about the girls, and she couldn't cheat them by denying them a foundation they might want later in life. They deserved the option of the values Markus was offering them.

"Will you come?" He held her gaze and she had to remind herself to speak. Had to force herself.

She cleared the ball of emotion from her throat—the emotion of self-discovery. Parenting was about far more than simply caring for the girls' physical needs or loving them.

"Of course, I'll come."

As if sensing her inner journey, Markus spoke with warmth. "It's just one of the many things we'll do together in making decisions about the girls' future. We've got so much to look forward to."

They had. Those things that, in the past, had frightened her and made her think about what she'd missed out on as a child, she could now give them to Phoebe and Zoë, and it filled her heart to bursting.

11

*M*arkus held his breath as Liv dressed Zoë. The ache in his chest finally passed and a new understanding lodged itself in his heart.

When this all began, it was a formality, the equation simple. Liv didn't have what it took to be a present, dedicated parent who could demonstrate her love in all the right ways. He'd accepted the responsibility Polly had asked him to carry, wholeheartedly. When he'd asked Liv to marry him, he'd expected her to throw her hands up, say it was all impossible and then leave when she understood how much he loved the girls. Now, things were so, so different.

Now, Liv was beginning to show all the traits of a dedicated parent—the all-night vigils, the baby balm, the rejection of him after they kissed—hell, she hadn't even been into town since she'd been here, except for the visit to the doctor. He didn't have the hold on the babies or Liv that he'd had in the beginning.

And now he loved all three of them.

But Liv didn't want that deep, passionate, soul searing love from him. And she'd said she never would while

Phoebe and Zoë were their top priority. Maybe organizing the christening, having Liv think about the deeper meaning behind what they were doing, would soften her distance from him.

He wanted to share something of himself with the girls, something of who he was, something of this wonderful time the four of them had spent together here. And if he could take Liv to the church to plan for the christening, it might give her some perspective on what they had together. That what they had was worth fighting for.

He added warm water to Phoebe's bath and then attempted to reconnect with Liv. "So you'll come to the church?" He checked the bath's temperature a final time, breathing deep Liv's lavender balm.

She looked up and smiled, slow enough and sincerely enough to make this hurt all the more, and his heart cracked open a little wider. "If it's that important to you, then of course I will. Where's the church?"

He cleared his throat and tried to sound sure and practical while his heart squeezed in his chest. "In the old part of Paphos. It's where my family have been going for generations." He placed Phoebe carefully in the bath, and she wriggled in delight as her body was covered with the perfumed water.

"Do you go regularly?" Liv was rocking in the chair with Zoë on her lap, her ringlets moving gently back and forth, the copper highlights shimmering in the pale light.

"I should." He busied himself with washing the baby so he wouldn't have to feel the cut of Liv's beauty. "I haven't been inside since my grandfather's funeral, just after I came back from France."

Her head snapped up and a shadow of pain washed over

her beautiful face. "I'm so sorry," she whispered. "I wish I'd been here for you."

He hadn't meant it like that. "It's okay, Liv," he said softly. "Having you here now is what counts."

The only sounds were the swish of water, as he finished washing Phoebe, and the rhythmic rocking of Liv with Zoë.

"It's a lovely idea, the christening," she finally said, as Markus lifted Phoebe out of the bath and patted her dry. "I think it's the right thing to do for the girls."

Markus stopped and lifted his gaze to hers. Something he hadn't seen since she arrived here, something heartfelt, radiated from the openness of her face and sent a jolt through him.

He gently pulled a brushed cotton nightgown over Phoebe's head, ordering himself not to read anything into Liv's expression. "Are you sure that's what Polly would've wanted?"

"I've been thinking a lot today, about what Polly might or might not have wanted, and the fact is we'll never know."

She stood and carried the sleeping Zoë to her crib. "I've been trying to carry out what I thought Polly's wishes would have been, and I truly believe she would have been proud of the way we've both handled things. And the way we're both going to be committed to their future. Christening the girls is a wonderful idea. A beautiful act of love and a wonderful start to their lives."

As she slowly bent her head and placed a kissed on the perfect face of the sleeping child, Markus hoped it could be a new beginning for all of them.

"Oh, hi. I hope this isn't a bad time."

Petro's hand gripped the half-open front door and he stared at Ana-Maria in horror.

Why did she always turn up so unexpectedly? It was nine in the morning and he had baby vomit down his shirt and was carrying a bucket of scraps for the compost. He yanked the apron from around his waist and threw it onto a coat stand beside the door.

Her face was flushed and without makeup, her glossy black hair was pulled back in a relaxed ponytail, her eyes twinkling and the thought that she was one of the most beautiful women he'd ever seen stamped itself indelibly inside his head like a tattoo.

"*Rizogalo*." The word came unbidden from his throat, and a grin tickled Ana-Maria's lips.

"Pardon me?"

"I have rice pudding cooking." He swung the door wide and waved her in, all rational thought draining from his brain. His palms slicked and his chest constricted. He hadn't had this reaction to a woman since his precious wife.

And he couldn't move. His legs had frozen, and he couldn't change his lips from the smile that was making his face begin to ache. "It burns very easily. The milk sticks on the bottom of the pan, and once it burns and catches you can't get rid of the scorched flavor."

He was rambling, raving.

The compost bin. It was heavy and stinky, and he was holding it while he looked at this vision of perfection.

He put it down and then realized a curl of melon skin was hanging out of it, juice dribbling on the floor.

"I'll get Markus for you."

"It's okay," she said. He couldn't look away from nut-brown eyes that sparkled. "No need to disturb him, but I've just received some important information that I said I'd get to Markus as soon as it arrived."

"It's good rice pudding. It won awards when my family had the restaurant. It won't be long." Maybe she'd stay? Maybe he'd put some pudding in a bowl for her, and he'd sit watching her eat it in the enthusiastic way she'd devoured his cheese pies?

She chuckled, and the light in her eyes traveled over her cheeks and brightened her already shining face. "You're tempting me," she said, and then looked down when color stained her cheeks.

He reached for the envelope that she passed to him and cleared his throat. "I hope it's good news."

She nodded and looked up again. "Let's say, it's news that will mean my involvement with this case will be over very soon."

He took a step back and nearly tripped on the bucket as his heart jolted. She wouldn't come here anymore? Wouldn't call? What if she decided she wanted to go back to Canada?

She shouldn't be the only unmarried sibling.

Where had that random thought come from?

He swallowed the rock in his throat and looked down at the melon juice pooling on the floor. "I see." Of course she wouldn't be coming anymore. Once custody was assigned to both Liv and Markus, Ana-Maria wouldn't need to have any more involvement.

"I'm sure Markus will let you know the decision, Petro. I can't really explain things as it's all confidential."

Heat burned his cheeks. "That's not what I was . . . I wasn't concerned . . . About those cooking lessons. If you have time . . . that is, if you're interested, I could give you some cooking lessons. Just the basics, the sort of thing you could impress your mother with."

She held his gaze and shot him a grin. "That would be lovely, Petro, really lovely."

His heart hitched in his chest as he stood staring at her in silence before he finally found his voice again. "Do you need to be anywhere? Markus has the girls and Liv's out for a walk. I was wondering if you might like to stay and have some rice pudding with me?"

She smiled a sweet, sweet smile and slowly nodded her head. "I'd love to." she said.

A few days later, Liv returned from a walk along the beach to find Markus working among the orchids in the internal courtyard. The girls had slept beautifully after their lavender bath the previous night and had only woken once in the night for a bottle. She'd felt so rested when they'd all woken at six that she'd decided to get some exercise.

The day was sparkling, and even from behind the glass, the intense sweetness of the vanilla pods Markus was harvesting seeped through her skin. Calm settled over her. A feeling that all was well with the world. She and Markus had been dealt a challenge, and they'd mustered their combined strength to work together and meet it.

They had the capacity to grow this unique little family, to feed and nurture it and build it into something they could all be a part of, and she felt proud of them both for putting aside their doubts and starting on that journey together.

She watched him through the glass—his body bending as he plucked the vanilla pods then placed them on a piece of bright white linen, the strong muscles in his back rippling beneath a thin blue T-shirt.

He straightened and moved to the stroller in the shade,

and pushed his sunglasses onto the top of his head, before crouching and talking to the girls in a soft, low voice. Liv could feel a smile building at the beautiful picture before her.

He was so happy being a father, so content with caring for the girls, that she didn't know why she'd ever imagined he wouldn't be this way. She'd been so wrapped up in what she'd needed before—how having his child would affect *her* —that she'd never considered he might change if he decided to take responsibility.

All she needed to do now was lock down tight her creeping desire for him, as well as her smoldering memories of him, so this feeling of contentment and safety could go on forever. But the growing power of her need for him sat like a spring in her chest that had curled even tighter when he'd said he'd wait for her. The more she fed her feelings, the higher the stakes for the girls became, and she couldn't risk it.

"Hey," she called as she opened a sliding door and moved toward him across the giant flagstones.

Markus immediately looked up and shot her a warm grin. "Hey," he said, then he turned back to Phoebe and Zoë. "Look who's here, girls."

The hot sweetness swirled around them as Liv bent down to the stroller too. "Hello, my darlings," she said, pulling aside the sunshade and being rewarded with two heart-melting smiles. "Who looks as though they had the best sleep in the world?"

"It really works, doesn't it? The lavender." Markus said beside her. The skin on his neck glistened with a light film of sweat, and she breathed in deep the citrus tang of him.

"You could start a whole cottage industry making baby balms if you wanted to," he said. "We could buy in some more lavender, and you could do soaps, lotions, all sorts. I could get you a new still set up in the shed. We could even use some of this vanilla." A perfect grin stole across his face.

Tension gripped her spine. "You mean you expect me to live in your house if we stay here?" Her heart began to pitch and roll, and she was glad of the sunglasses covering her eyes. They hadn't talked about any arrangements beyond the marriage to ensure Liv could stay here.

He stood. "Work from here anyway." He moved to the next plant and began searching for a pod. "We can see how things develop, but there are a number of options. We can live in the city house during the week and come down here at weekends. That way you can be with the girls while I'm at work during the week, and we can spend weekends down here for you to work on your baby balms while I look after the girls during the day."

Liv chewed her lip. "I hadn't imagined we'd live in the same house," she said, hesitating. "I thought I'd get a place close by so we could both have our independence." Her voice began to trip. If they were sharing a house, how would she keep enough distance from him until he understood nothing could happen between them?

He wiped his arm across his forehead, his tricep flexing with the movement, and his face tightened. "We don't have to, but I wouldn't like to think of the girls being moved around all the time. It'd be better if they stayed in one place and we came to them. The west wing of this house is fully self-contained, as is the upstairs of my city house. There's no reason why we couldn't share the houses and still have our own space."

Liv breathed a quiet sigh of relief. For a moment, she'd been afraid he'd say the thing about waiting for her again, but his ready solution calmed her worry. He was pulling away from her and the knowledge caused a tug of bitter-sweet loss. And relief.

"Maybe we could work something out where the girls stay in one place and we take turns living in the house."

He speared her with a look of disbelief. "You really think we need to resort to that?"

"What'll people think," she said, trying to deflect his disapproval of her idea. "Petro, your friends and family. What will they say about us bringing up the girls together without . . ." She stopped, not quite sure how to say it.

"They'll see that we both love the girls. That nothing's more important than that."

Liv turned back to the girls and reached out a hand to Phoebe. The little girl wrapped a tiny finger around her ring finger. Maybe it would be best to bring them up in the same house, in the meantime anyway, while they were so little, needing to be fed so much in the day and night. It made perfect, logical sense, and Markus was obviously thinking that way too. He was different. More relaxed. As if he'd accepted this arrangement now and had put any fantasies of being together aside.

"So, if we're going to see the priest soon, you'd better tell me more about the christening ceremony," she said as she watched him gently pull a vanilla pod from a vine. "When should we have it?"

He smiled. "I've been thinking we should really wait until my mom arrives. She booked tickets as soon as she could get time off work, and she'll be here next month. She'd love to be involved. She'll be especially pleased that Polly gave the girls Greek names."

"Really?" Liv was astonished. "Phoebe and Zoë are Greek?"

"Yes. Zoë means life and Phoebe comes from the word

for bright, although in mythology she's associated with the moon."

Liv thought back to something she'd read about the legend of Aphrodite's rock and the moon. She couldn't remember the details, and would Google it later, but it was amazing that Polly had given the girls a link to this place.

"We'll need to choose godparents, too," Markus said. "They're a very important part of the ceremony. When we adopt the girls, you'll be out of a job as their nona."

The thought hit Liv swift and hot. She wouldn't be Phoebe and Zoë's godmother now, she'd be their mother, and Markus would be their father, when they eventually adopted them. She swallowed back the increasing lump in her throat and reached out to Zoë, who also clung to one of her fingers.

"Who would you choose as godparents?" Liv asked. "Family? Friends? Do they have to be Greek?"

Markus dropped his voice to a whisper and held her gaze. "I can think of someone we both know who loves the girls and who'd want to be in their life."

"Petro!" Liv exclaimed, then lowered her voice too. "Oh, Markus that would be perfect! When do you think we could go ahead with it?"

"It'll take a while to organize, but I'd think in a couple of weeks. And by then, we'll also have worked out how we'll go about getting married."

Liv swallowed. "I guess there's no real rush for that either, except of course it will need to happen before my entry visa runs out."

"It would be nice if we could christen the girls after we get married," Markus ventured.

Liv bent her head and stared hard at one of the paving stones. Everything was happening so quickly—talk of where they'd live, christenings and marriages. With a smile stitched to her face, she turned back to him. "Let's just take things slowly, shall we? There's no rush in the meantime."

Markus reached into his back pocket and pulled out an envelope. "This came earlier," he said. "Special delivery from Ana-Maria. Nicer than an email, I guess."

He waited until she'd freed her fingers from the babies' clutches and then handed her the envelope, and she saw an official-looking crest in the top left corner.

Her heart slammed against her breastbone. The paternity results.

"I asked them to send the results in Greek and English," he said, smiling, "so you wouldn't have to take my word for it."

With fumbling fingers, Liv opened the envelope and scanned one of the pages inside. She only needed to read one sentence:

DNA testing indicates, to an accuracy of one hundred percent, that Markus Leonidas Panos is not the father of the twin girls in question.

Relief coursed through her body, and she was sideswiped by the force of her reaction. She'd believed Markus when he'd told her he wasn't Phoebe and Zoë's father, but the confirmation banished the last nagging fragments of doubt. She turned to him as she screwed the piece of paper into a tight little ball in her fist.

"What are you doing?" he asked, his eyes growing wide.

"Well, it's not true, is it?" Liv said, trying to stop the twitch at the corner of her mouth.

Markus placed the pruning shears on the ground and held her stare, his face dropping as he took a step toward her. "Of course, it's true, Liv. It's there in black and white. I'm not the girls' father."

"Of course, you are," she said as she stood and put her hands on her hips. "Anyone can see that you are."

He took two more steps until he was close enough that she could feel the heat from his body, inhale the tang of sweat from working in the sun. Teasing was fun, but it made her heart race in unexpected ways to have Markus standing so close, indignant and strong.

"Liv, I told you, Polly and I didn't . . . I never would've . . ."

She started to laugh, and as she reached out a hand to touch his arm, relief washed over his face. "What I meant," she said, smiling as she spoke, "is that this piece of paper says you're not Phoebe and Zoë's biological father, but in all the ways that count you are their father."

"Thank you," he said, his voice rich and low.

"I mean it," she said. She let her hand drop, wanting him to know that these words came from the deepest part of her, not a part filled with desire and desperation, but a part filled with respect and admiration. "No one deserves to be Phoebe and Zoë's father more than you do, and nobody but the girls deserve such a wonderful man to be their dad."

The way he smiled at her made her heart sing.

Liv held her breath as they climbed the steps to the huge beige church the next week. Its domed roof seemed to hold up the perfect blue sky and its small arched windows hinted it would be an escape from the searing heat of the day.

Markus held the door open and shot her a heart-warming grin as she moved past him. Once inside, she took deep breaths as her senses were assaulted by the ancient smells from within. Calming waves of incense washed over her in a gentle rhythm as she moved from the bright, warm day to the cool, dark belly of the church and had to squint until her eyes became adjusted to the dim light.

And then she held her breath again to keep from crying out in wonder.

It was as if she'd been transported back to the pages of some magical fairy-tale book. All around the walls, candles burned in trays of sand, their flickering glow passing soft shadows across the brilliant gold pictures of saints hanging everywhere.

Markus reached out a hand to guide her forward, and she rejoiced in the togetherness of this moment as his palm spread solid across her back. She'd never been anywhere like this, and she didn't want to do anything wrong or make a mistake. Turning to Markus, she raised her eyebrows in silent question.

He bent to whisper in her ear, and the feathered touch of his breath against her skin sent a million goose bumps all over her.

"Just do what I do," he said.

She followed him as he put a coin in a box and picked up two long thin candles. He then lit them from those already burning and placed them in the sand. "One for our Phoebe, one for our Zoë," he said quietly, and Liv's heart lurched in her chest. The power of his voice, his unspoken love for the girls, touched her soul deep. Pride and wonder that they were now united for one sublime purpose ran sweetly through her veins. She wouldn't feel regret that it meant they couldn't really be together. She'd find solace in the depth of their shared vision, in the future that they'd be working toward together every single day.

He bent and kissed the glass cover of the exquisite silver icon, and Liv did the same. From somewhere inside, she felt

Polly's presence, Polly's acceptance of what they were about to plan, and it stilled her heart for a moment.

Markus indicated a pew at the rear of the church, and they moved toward it. There was no service being conducted, but there were a number of older men and women inside, some in groups whispering and chattering, some on their own, and a woman was dusting a table at the front.

"This is amazing," Liv whispered as she sat close to Markus, feeling the power of his body beside her. This place was such a part of who he was, part of the whole of him that she'd missed for so long. "Should we have brought the girls so the priest could meet them instead of leaving them with Petro?"

"No." His tone was soft. "We'll bring them to a Sunday service sometime before the christening so he can meet them then." He looked around them. "It's beautiful, isn't it? I spent a lot of time here with my parents and my brothers. Not always valuing it as I do now." He grinned at her, pride shining in his voice.

"Is this where they'd get christened?" she managed to ask. "Up the front?"

He nodded. "The whole ceremony takes about an hour, and it's quite involved. There's a ritual of anointing with oil, cutting the first locks of hair, and of course, immersing them in the water. The godparents we've chosen will play a big part in the ceremony. They'll have bought the girls new clothes to be dressed in after they've been christened and a gold cross to wear around their necks."

"It sounds beautiful," Liv breathed.

Markus watched Liv's eyes dart around the inside of the church. At one point she looked right up to the ceiling, and the pale skin at her throat stretched so thin he could see the delicate veins in her neck, which made him burn to kiss her there. He wanted to drag her into his arms and tell her she could stop pretending.

He could see she was affected by being here. The distance she'd been keeping was softening. He didn't know how much longer he could wait before he told her of his feelings, but he'd made a promise that he'd wait for her and not rush her into anything she wasn't ready for. In truth, though, it was unmitigated torture pretending he could do this all as friends.

"I'd always imagined being married in this church."

Liv was silent for a moment as she twisted the fabric of her skirt around her finger. "And now, the first time you get married it'll be in a civil ceremony in the mayor's office."

"The first time? You think I'll get married again?"

"Of course, you will." Her voice was a rasping whisper. "I'm sure you'll get to experience a real marriage one day."

A real marriage. Disappointment and confusion ripped through his body. She really believed there was no future for them? That once they were married and she could stay in the country, he'd just toss her aside to go and find someone else?

"There won't be anyone else," he said quietly.

He heard the tight sigh escape from her lips. "Of course, there will, Markus. I won't hold you back from finding someone special. Once you and I have sorted out how every-thing will work with the girls, when we're sure their lives are stable and secure, we can look to our own happiness."

She slowly shook her head and took his hand in hers. Her touch was as light as breath across his skin.

"I'll be part of your life, forever, Markus. I won't go away like I did before. But that doesn't mean you need to deny yourself what will make you happy."

He bit down on the desire to tell her there would be no one else, *could* be no one else, because she was the only one who would make him happy.

"You and I have Phoebe and Zoë as our glue now. We'll be together at their sixteenth birthday parties, their graduations, and even, god willing," she said as she looked around the walls once more, "their weddings in a place like this. We won't lose each other this time because we're bonded by something bigger than ourselves. And the beautiful thing is that because we won't be lovers, because we won't hurt each other in the same ways we did before, we can always be part of each other's and the girls' lives."

Blood chilled in his veins. She really meant this.

He'd thought she was just holding back, trying to be strong, in the wake of all the emotion that was swirling about them. Trying to put her needs and desires second to the commitment he could see she so genuinely had. But they were in a church. She had to be telling the truth.

He'd given her every opportunity to open up to him, to tell him what she was afraid of and what they'd need to do to make a success of their love this time, but she was doing none of that. She was pulling down the shutters on even the possibility of something developing between them.

"Let's just focus on the christening now, Markus." She placed his hand back in his lap and looked around for the priest.

If waiting wouldn't work, then he'd have to think of another way to convince her.

12

―――――

$\mathcal{L}$ater that evening, when the girls were asleep, Liv walked toward the living room to fold more washing.

It had been a beautiful afternoon at the church, and they'd decided on a ceremony in a month's time when Markus's mom would be here from Brentwood Bay and would have an opportunity to be involved in the preparations. Markus had talked of aunts and cousins he'd like to invite as well, and the possibility of the girls growing up surrounded by a precious extended family wherever they lived thrilled Liv.

Although she'd felt Markus's pain at being in the church and speaking of the practicalities of their own marriage, she'd employed every rational and reasonable phrase to pull back from him again. But it was excruciating. The closer he tried to get, and the more she felt her need for him grow, the more frightened she became about how this would all end.

He was tidying in the living room when she entered.

He looked up. "Glass of wine?"

"Yes, thanks." She pushed a ringlet from her forehead,

and when he passed her a glass of red, she walked to the picture windows and looked out on the darkening night.

"I think Polly would've approved of what we did today," she said. "She'd have thought the church was exquisite, and she'd have loved the priest."

"Father Paul is a good man," Markus said as he folded a tiny blanket. "I didn't tell him the girls weren't ours, because custody hasn't been finalized, but I'm sure he'll be supportive when he knows the truth." He looked across to her. "I'm glad you think Polly would've liked what we're doing."

An image of Polly and Markus talking in Polly's final hours lay heavy in Liv's mind. She'd never asked what they'd discussed or what he'd thought when Polly asked him to help her.

"What was it like when Polly contacted you?" She ventured. "It must've been quite a shock to hear from her after all that time. I guess the last time you saw her would have been when she stayed with us in Paris." She swallowed the lump in her throat that was always there when she spoke about her best friend. "I know she was upset when you and I broke up."

Markus opened the French doors wider and gestured for her to move to the table outside. Small bowls were laid out on the table with a gauze throw over the top to deter insects.

A plump moon, not quite full, shone above the bay in the balmy night air and turned the sea a brilliant silver around the rocks that rose like waking giants from the deep. The beauty touched her deeply, the way it had when she'd first arrived, and a centering calm fell over her that this place would be a part of her now, a part of all four of them.

Her heart and body stirred at the sound of Markus's deep voice so close. "She did think we'd been good together.

She talked about it a lot. Even when she first called and asked me to help her with legal advice, she said she thought it was wrong that you and I weren't still together."

Liv held her glass tighter and tried to still the tremble inside at the thought of him sharing Polly's final words.

She nodded. "She kept telling me you were the one and that I'd made a mistake in leaving you." Her brain scrambled with the honesty of her admission.

His mouth quirked in a grin. "But you didn't take her advice." The thump in her heart was too strong for her to smile back as his gaze held her. He looked serious again. "Feel like some food?"

Together they pulled chairs to the table, and after she was seated, he moved next to her and they both looked out to sea.

He breathed deeply as he took off his jacket and threw it across the outdoor couch. "It's got so hot. Smell the orange blossom? It's amazing how it intensifies in the evenings."

She turned to him. "You can smell that? From all the way up here?"

He was reaching for one of the bowls, but he stopped and looked straight at her for a moment then nodded. Something she couldn't read crossed his face.

He lifted out a small pastry and held it up. "*Mezzethes*. Lots of tastes. A Cypriot tradition." His lips lifted in a grin. "Petro gave up making things for me for a long time because I'd lost my taste for most things, but he's been cooking up a storm since you've been here. He says that in the last few weeks this place has been much happier. I've even seen him looking in some of those baby books for what he can cook up for the girls when they start to eat solid food."

Liv laughed. "He's so lovely. I was a bit scared of him when I first arrived, but now I can see how much he loves working for you and loves having the girls around. I even think he's taken a bit of a shine to Ana-Maria."

Markus grinned. "He invited her in for rice pudding. I've never seen him look so nervous."

Liv clapped her hands together. "Oh, that's so sweet."

"It would be great if he found someone. His four children live all over the world now, so he doesn't get to see them very often," Markus said. "Now, open up."

The intimacy of his words, his movement, the promise of a connection, caused her to avert her eyes as she parted her lips. She had to remember her plan—the longer she could keep from being close to him, the easier it would be for her feelings to fade away. But the sweet pressure of his fingers so close to her lips scrambled her thoughts.

Heat lasered from his eyes to her skin, and she tried to ignore the explosion in her heart and deny the depth charge rippling through her.

Time. All she needed was time to get used to being with him again, and then she could get these feelings under control. She bit down on the pie, and tangy cheese with piquant herbs melted in her mouth.

"Good?" He whispered.

"Mmmmm." It was all she could manage.

"Try one of these olives." His bicep stretched, the thin cotton of his T-shirt clinging to the taut, well defined muscle, as he reached for another bowl. "Petro pickles them himself."

"You said you'd lost your sense, even your desire, for taste and smell." She reached into the bowl before he could pull one out for her, at the same time trying to quell the shaking of her hand and the shiver in her heart. She couldn't avoid this sort of time with him, and she needed to train herself to ignore the reactions of old and focus on the practicalities of the future.

"It's come back in the last couple of weeks." His voice was still low, and Liv had to use every ounce of willpower not to meet his gaze. "Came back just as quickly as it went away."

She took a bite of the tangy olive and ordered her body to pull itself together and stop giving off unwarranted signals.

"I'll be able to start making the vanilla essence soon." She turned to him, straining to have the sensual spell broken for a moment so her giddy mind could get back on track. "If that works out, I could try and use some of the other plants you've got in the garden, and maybe we could plant some bergamot and chamomile."

They were both quiet for some time, and Liv started to relax as she let her senses be filled with the food in front of them, the wafts of lavender and orange blossom from the garden, and the rhythmic hush-hush of the waves on the sand below. It was like so many nights they'd spent in the past, bathing in the beauty of things that surrounded them. But this time they were friends. Friends with a shared purpose who just needed to learn how to communicate to be together again.

Finally, Markus broke the silence. "Is there something you wanted to ask me?"

Liv turned her head toward him, perplexed. "What do you mean?"

"You started asking about Polly. About what I thought when she contacted me out of the blue. Did you want to know what Polly and I spoke about?" He cleared his throat. "Before she died. I've wanted to tell you, but I wasn't sure how raw all of it still was for you or how much you'd want to know."

Liv pressed her spine hard into the back of the chair and rubbed her hands across her eyes. She did want to know what Polly had been feeling and thinking in her last days.

"I suppose." She tried to keep her voice steady. "I mean . . . it doesn't change anything." She made her words sharper in an effort to cover the emotion that was building inside. "I know how much Polly loved me and how hard it must have been for her that I couldn't find her, couldn't get to her in time."

Markus shifted his whole body until he was facing her. "She'd hesitated about telling you she'd come to Cyprus—didn't want the fact that she'd been talking to me upset you. She was going to text you on the day she became so ill but obviously didn't get the chance. Do you want to know what she said about you and me?"

Raw emotion took over before Liv had a chance to disguise it. No, her heart said, but "Yes," her mouth blurted in a jagged whisper.

He was silent for a moment, and the only sounds were the fall of the waves in the distance and the scrape as he moved his boot backward and forward on the decking. He cleared his throat. "She told me what she thought of us breaking up. Said what she thought of me."

A grin tugged at Liv's lips as she imagined Polly being blunt with Markus about what had happened between them. Polly had always believed in the truth, in calling a spade a spade. Life had been tougher for her than for most people, and she didn't believe in wasting time on pleasantries and platitudes. "What did she say?"

Markus stared out to sea. "She said if I'd really loved you, I'd have made you change your mind."

His Adam's apple moved as he swallowed. "She said if I didn't follow you, didn't beg you to come back when you left, if I wouldn't move heaven and earth for you, then maybe it wasn't real love."

Liv gasped. "Oh, Markus." Her words left her lips in a whisper. "Why would she have said that? Why would she think you could change things?"

He didn't answer; his gaze fixed on the table in front of them.

"What did you say to her?"

Why didn't you fight for me?

Maybe if he gave her the answer to that question, she could truly move on.

"I said she was wrong. I said I loved you as deeply as I could, but it wasn't enough." His gaze flicked up to her. "Now I know that's not true."

Her chest hollowed. "What's not true?"

He clenched a fist on the tabletop. "What I thought I had with you was an illusion, and now I've seen the real thing I can't believe I was so blind."

She shook her head, praying he wouldn't say any of this, but desperate to hear it anyway.

His tone remained low and sensual and it purred through her body. "Let me explain it another way." He nodded out to sea. "Do you know the legend of the rocks?"

Relieved to be pulled away from the intimacy of the conversation, Liv managed a shaking smile. "Yes, you said that Aphrodite was born from the foam around the rock."

"But I didn't tell you the rest."

He paused then, and his hot stare burned a trail over her skin, heating her blood. As if he held some magnetic pull for her—she had to look at him. "So, tell me."

His eyes held her. No light sparked from them, just deep,

dark mystery and passion dredged from their depths. "Legend says that if you swim three times around it naked at the full moon, you'll have everlasting love and everlasting life."

Despite the serious way he watched her, Liv bit her lip and raised an eyebrow to try to suggest a calm detachment, but in truth it was as if her insides had liquefied. "Polly would've loved a story like that."

"On full moon nights like this," he said, innuendo dancing around them, "if you make the swim, you're guaranteed Aphrodite's protection."

She couldn't help imagining Markus's hard, wet body pulling muscular strokes through the moonlit water while an image of her danced in his head. "But it's so big, that rock," Liv said, trying to slow her heart. "You'd be exhausted."

"No." He leaned his forearms on the table. "You've made the classic mistake. And this is what I've learned since you've been here."

She still didn't understand. The intensity of his gaze sent a shiver skating across her skin, and although her mind warned against hearing more, she had to ask him. "What do you mean?"

Markus turned and stared straight ahead. "What makes you think the largest rock is Aphrodite's?"

She tilted her head and tried to get him to look at her. "I don't know." She laughed, intrigued that she'd jumped to conclusions. "I guess I thought if it's a landmark, and if the goddess of love was born from it, then it made sense it was the biggest one."

"All the tourists think so too." Finally, he turned his face to her, but there was no amused expression or teasing smile. His face was serious intent laced with unmistakable desire.

"I see them down there, posing in front of the huge rock, when in fact many locals believe the *real* Aphrodite's rock is a tiny one, almost hidden in the middle of the bay."

Liv swallowed. She knew what was coming, but she asked the question anyway. "Why are you telling me all this, Markus?"

"I want you to understand how I feel about you now, Liv." The light, deep in his eyes, burned brighter as he spoke. "I thought what we had back then was real. I thought I loved you in the right ways, the ways that really counted. But how could it have been real if I wasn't listening to what you needed? I wanted children with you but didn't see that I had to change before that could happen.

"When you left, I believed you didn't have the capacity for love and commitment because you weren't listening to what I needed. If I'd known what was closest to your heart all along—the desire to show love and commitment in a safe and stable environment—things could've been different."

The look in his eyes ignited her skin, and the ensuing heat was pushing into her core as he continued. "We've come such a long way, Liv. Things can be different this time."

She couldn't speak, was too busy trying to ignore the effect his honesty was having deep within her. Did he really mean this, or was it just more of the same to get her to stay?

"Since you've been here, I've seen your capacity for love every day. When I watch you being a mother to Phoebe and Zoë, it does something to me that I've never experienced before."

"So, you trust me now?" she asked, her heart lurching. "You think I have what it takes to be here for the girls forever?"

"If I'd truly understood why you walked out before, if I'd

understood how selfless you were being in the past, I would never have had those doubts."

Each muscle in Liv's body released the tension she'd been carrying since she'd arrived here. "I'm so glad, Markus," she said, her voice quavering as she looked at him. "It's important to me that you believe I'll be a good mother and that we can put our old feelings away and concentrate on forming a whole new relationship."

His spine straightened. "I didn't say anything about putting old feelings away." His voice was as low and dangerous as it had been the day he'd brushed his lips across hers and she'd succumbed . . .

She bit her lip, not wanting to break the spell of this vision, but needing to put a stop to any expectations. "Old feelings *have* to be put away, Markus. You don't have to pretend anymore. I'm not going anywhere. I've already told you that I don't have faith that anything could be different between you and me in the future, and I'm not prepared to ever risk the girls losing another parent."

"You'd sacrifice your happiness for the belief that you and I couldn't make a relationship work?"

"I've done it before," she said, trying desperately to keep a distance. "And the result was that you and I didn't bring a child into the world who might have lost a parent the way I did."

"You don't love me?"

Four stark words flew across the table and wrapped tight around her as Markus reached a hand out and placed it inches from her own fingers. The air pulsed and burned with his anticipation of an answer.

"You can look me in the eye and say that kiss we shared in my office wasn't real? That when I felt you melting in my arms it wasn't because you wanted me?" His voice dropped to a husky whisper. "That since you've been here you haven't imagined us making love, being together again in every way?"

His questions hummed inside her head, and in a panic, Liv willed herself to respond so he wouldn't have any doubts about what she could give him in their future. For the very first time since she'd arrived here, she was beginning to wonder if his feelings for her were real after all. And it scared the life out of her.

She let her gaze meet his and held firm. Her heartbeat spiked as she rehearsed in her head the words that had to be said, and then she willed her voice to be strong. "Of course, I love you, Markus. I've *always* loved you. But love's just not enough."

"Love *is* enough."

His pupils dilated and his body tensed, as if he was about to move toward her, but she carried on so that this time he'd understand her completely. This was the point of no return, the moment they both had to live through before their past could be put behind them forever.

"We've been in love before, and it wasn't enough to over-come the doubts we had about each other. And now we have another two people in the mix. Two little people who don't deserve for us to try and fail. The fundamental thing that will always overshadow that love, always override it, can never be undone. I left you when things got tough in our relationship, and you'd have every right to wonder when I would do that again. And to be honest, *I'd* wonder if I'd do that again. We need to acknowledge that and accept it, but we also need to turn it into something that's going to make our lives, and the lives of the girls, all the richer."

She stood, wanting to put some distance between her words and the deep desire in his eyes. She moved away from the table and across to the edge of the decking. The heat in his gaze melted the skin on her back.

"You're not ready," he said quietly from the table. "I understand that."

"It's not that I'm not ready, Markus," she said, turning back to him. "It's that I've made a conscious decision that a relationship with you can't be a part of my being here. My being married to you for the girls' security won't be a trial or an experiment. It will be me making a commitment forever, so I can be a mother to the girls forever. And I can't have old desires jeopardizing that." Oh, god, how she wanted to turn and run from the doubt in her heart and the pull of his body. Why did this have to be so hard? So impossible?

He was quiet.

"Do you understand what I mean?"

"Of course, I do." He sat back a little. "You're making the girls your priority, as you should, but in time I know you'll acknowledge the feelings you still have for me."

Liv closed her eyes. "What makes you believe in us so much, Markus? Why do you have such faith that I'll come back to you? That I'll put all my pledges to the girls aside and say I want to try again?"

When she opened her eyes, the burn of his stare sizzled on her cheeks. "You really want to know?" Sensual confidence melded with his words as he stood and took a step toward her.

"Yes," she said, feeling the sweet threat of him moving closer. "I don't understand why you feel this way when I've given you no encouragement."

He said nothing as he took another step closer, so he was only a touch away. Slowly, he lifted his hand and grazed it the length of her arm.

The shiver reached the deepest organs in her body, and

it didn't escape Markus's notice. "There," he said, pointing to the soft hairs on her arm that had risen under his touch. "That's how I know you're not telling the truth. Those tiny bumps up your arm tell me it's all still there; the way you feel about me is all still real."

He moved closer and she tensed her body, determined that once she got through tonight, proved to him that her reactions didn't matter, that he didn't need to do this to make her stay here, then this would never happen again. "That's not enough of a reason," she said, her voice fracturing.

"Then maybe you need another." He stepped infinitesimally closer so that the heat from his body surrounded her and the scent that had the capacity to calm was now sending her nerve endings into overdrive. He leaned his face closer, until the warmth of his breath played across her cheek, and she gasped.

He moved his face away, but he trailed a finger down the cheek his breath had caressed. "Your skin was pale a moment ago," he said softly. "Now it's pink, and I can imagine how that color's traveling down your neck, across your hidden skin . . ."

Liv pulled in a breath but couldn't make herself meet his gaze. "You're not playing fair, Markus. You're not thinking things through."

"Still not enough proof?" he asked. "I know I said I'd wait until you came to me, but if you really want evidence then I'll have to show you."

His heated whisper was warm against her neck seconds before he bent his head and pressed his lips to hers, and despite the agreement she had with herself, despite knowing this could put everything in jeopardy, she couldn't stop herself melting into his kiss.

Drugged by the release of her body, her limbs turned liquid as Markus trailed his hands up her bare arms, leaving goose bumps in their wake, and then pulled her to him. "I know how hard it's been for you. I know the last thing you wanted was to see me again . . . but I've never stopped loving you, Liv. And now that I know what really happened to us back then, I know that love is enough to get us through."

He drew her around until she faced his warm, broad chest, and then he lifted her chin with a finger. "I know you still feel the same about me because I can taste it in your kiss."

He kissed her again, and this time the kiss was an affirmation, a salve for the confusion racing around Liv's head. A groan, more primal than sensual, left Markus's throat, and he leaned into her until their bodies joined.

He trailed a line of kisses from the corner of her mouth down to the hollow of her throat, until a fire began there and rushed to her core, causing a rope of breath to leave her lips.

But just as the fire inside her was taking hold, he stopped and looked her straight in the eyes. "That kiss is why I know we'll be together, Liv."

13

She could've pushed him away then, held his face softly in her hands, eased him from her, and said this was far enough, that letting things progress from here would be a monumental mistake.

But she didn't.

Instead, she twined her fingers through his glossy black waves and held his face, before guiding his lips across her skin. Letting every cell of her body that had been aching for him since she'd arrived here have its release. The moist warmth of his lips on her hungry body mirrored the burning racing through her veins, and she leaned into him desire building as she melted.

"Liv, Liv." He whispered her name between kisses as he traced a finger along the top of her dress then teased across her shoulders, pushing the straps down as they got in his way.

His gaze burned into hers, before she dragged him to her once more and kissed him hungrily. She pulled his T-shirt from his pants and ran her fingers across the warm skin at his waist. Memories of making love to him rocketed through her and the muscles low in her abdomen pulled tight. His smell, his warmth and the firmness of his kiss were all just as she'd remembered and ached for so many times.

Desperate to feel more of him on her, she dragged his T-shirt up, and he stopped kissing her long enough to help its journey over his head.

Now his bronze chest, lit only by the moon and the lights from inside, was in touching, kissing distance, and she trailed one finger down the length of it, his abdominal muscles dancing as she moved her touch across them slowly.

"Markus," she breathed, before placing both palms flat on his chest and kissing every scrap of him she could lay claim to.

"Slow, my darling, slow," he whispered, and guided her back toward the couch. "I want to see you first." His voice was graveled and strained.

As he stood before her, the moon shadowed by his tall frame, the promise of his body kicked deep and delicious goose bumps swept her from head to foot. Then he knelt down, and for a moment she was blinded by the brilliance of the moon.

And in that second, the warnings began again, whispering in her ears, chattering about consequences and regrets, but as she looked down at his ebony hair, his squared shoulders and bare, broad back, she felt the caress of his palm from her ankle, up the inside of her leg, and she drowned those whispers in a groan of her own.

"God, you're gorgeous," he whispered, before pulling her closer so their bodies melded, then easing her back onto the pillowy softness of the couch.

Warm sparks blossomed from her chest and moved

rapid-fire out to the tips of her fingers and toes, and pulsed in her core.

"I can't wait." She barely managed to push the words out through parched lips. "I want to feel all of you." Markus stepped back and wrenched his belt off, then in two simple flicks his buttons were undone and he was standing in his boxers.

She reached up and pulled him down to her. Squeezing her eyes closed, she fought back the tears that stung her lids. Bittersweet pleasure raked her body at the feeling of his skin against hers, his body joining with her own and the thousand kisses he was showering across her face. This was it, the moment she had so desperately wanted, and the moment that would bring an end to everything.

When they were spent, he whispered her name, and she could feel the tears begin to pinch the back of her nose but didn't stop them.

She eased him back so he could see her face. Maybe if he could see how much this frightened her, he'd see what she'd failed to show him until now.

"Are you okay?" He said, a small frown marring his forehead.

"I'm fine," she said as she eased him back and sat up. She crossed both arms around her body as if she could hold her organs together.

He knelt beside her and the night breeze suddenly became cool against her skin. "Liv, what's wrong?"

"This," she said in a strangled whisper. "What we've just done."

"But you wanted to," he said, tilted her chin so she had to look at him. "I could feel it in your body, in your response. Don't say this was a mistake, Liv."

She gazed up at him, sorrow dragging through her veins. "I wish it wasn't," she said softly. "I wish it wasn't."

"It's not. How can it be when we both make each other feel like this?"

"We've always made each other feel like this, Markus, that's never gone away, and that's the problem, don't you see? I don't think I can stay here, Markus. If you want me this much and can't truly have me, then nothing can work for us as a family. We'd be running on bitterness and regret, and the girls would see and feel that every day.

He smiled and it pierced her heart. "But this is like the story of the rocks, Liv. What we had before was an illusion, a false belief. What we have now is the real thing and we can't fight it."

She shrugged and looked straight in his eyes. "We can't fight it, and we can't ignore it and it's going to lead us into the same mess we've been in before. I thought I could pretend it all away, that if I didn't get close enough to you, we could move our relationship to a different level."

"Don't do this to me, Liv."

"That's just it, Markus. I don't *want* to do this to you." She sat up straighter. "I don't want to do it to us, to the girls, but I know we can't be together. We've hurt each other too much. This makes me question whether I might run out again. That's no sort of environment to bring Phoebe and Zoë up in. And apart from all that, I don't want to keep pushing you away. Every time you say you'll wait for me, or that it's only a matter of time, just reminds me that I could hurt you as much as I did before."

"Then why did you make love to me?" The hurt in his voice made her heart squeeze. He stood up and walked toward the edge of the deck, and she followed.

"Because I put me and my needs first. Not yours. Not

Phoebe's and Zoë's. I put my immediate needs before the future of all of us, and I can't, and *won't*, let that happen again."

"You just need to have faith, Liv." He scrubbed his hands through his hair. "Have faith that you and I have changed. That we won't do to each other what we did before. That I won't scare you and you won't run out on me."

"Faith's not enough, Markus. I can't gamble the security of two little girls on faith."

"I'll wait until you can."

I'm hurting him all over again.

The thought wove itself so tight in Liv's mind that she could feel the ache in her temples. He didn't get it; he didn't want to see what she'd been trying to warn him against all along.

How could she stay here when pushing him away would make him as devastated as he'd been before? God, if he truly didn't see how much they could hurt each other, then they couldn't be in the same town, let alone the same house.

"Stop this, Markus," she said desperately. "Please stop doing this, because I don't know where it will end. I don't trust myself. I don't trust that this pressure won't make me run again."

There, she'd said it, said the thing that had been buried so deep within her. Running was all she knew, all she'd done her whole life since she lost her parents. She had no faith that she wouldn't do it again.

"It will end where we both want it to end," he said swiftly. "Living and loving together as we should be."

"No. If you can't see how impossible it is for us ever to be together, then I'll have to change my mind. I'll have to say no to your proposal and take the girls back to Brentwood Bay as I'd always planned."

A muscle jumped in his jaw, cutting the smooth surface of his skin.

"You have to promise you'll stay away from me from now on, that this is the last time we'll fall over the edge. If you can't do that, then I'll have no choice but to leave and take the girls with me."

14

The next morning, Liv could feel something coiled within Markus, something he wanted to get off his chest, and the tight, concerned look on his face alarmed her. Was he about to agree with her ultimatum last night?

Her eyes burned from the tears she'd cried alone in her bed while her head thumped with anguish that they could never be together.

She wished with all her heart that what he'd said to her was true—that his love for her was born out of an understanding that she'd changed and that he wanted to be with her and that she wouldn't run out on him and the girls when it all got too much—but still her doubts remained.

She couldn't trust she wouldn't take fright and leave like she'd done before, and that's what cut to her core. Remove the doubt and indecision, the prospect of hurting him all over again when they were in too deep. She had get him to agree to give up his custody claim. Better she hurt him now than when the girls really knew what they'd be losing.

Every cell in her body tensed. "Markus, what is—"

"Get your shoes on, Liv. Petro has the girls. We're going down to the rock."

"But we . . . My robe . . ."

He held up a hand. "Please."

He waited for her outside, and when she came to him, the look on his face had softened, and the light in his eyes held a spark she'd seen when he'd touched her last night.

As he reached for her hand, she hesitated for a moment then shook the worry from her mind and slipped her hand into his. This was it. He'd realized what he surely must have known in his heart all along, that their time together had passed. That he could stop believing in her and promise to give up his dream that they'd be together.

When they reached the beach, the sun was rising in the sky. Warm pillows of air sat around Liv's body and the briny smell of the sea invaded her senses.

Markus dropped her hand and turned to face her.

"It's okay, Markus," she said, her heart pounding.

Slowly he pushed his sunglasses up on his head, revealing the endless coffee eyes that still seemed to know her innermost thoughts. "I won't let you leave, Liv," he said. "I'll do what it takes to make you stay."

Naked relief flourished through her body. He'd realized that they could never be together and something inside her died at the thought.

"I realized something yesterday," he said quietly but firmly.

He'd listened to her last night. He was going to agree that nothing more could happen between them. She was tempted to interrupt, to tell him she could understand how hard having her around while he tried to make a new life would be for him, but she wanted to hear it in his own words.

"Tell me," she said.

He thrust his hands in both his pockets and Liv wondered for a crazy minute if he was nervous.

"I could never have believed this day would come," he said. "A day when I felt as though what happened between you and me in the past was a blessing. But now I can see that what we went through in Paris has made us stronger people. It defined what's most important for us and what we want in our lives."

She bit her lip. "I don't understand."

"I know I said I'd wait until you came to me, but I've seen in the past few days that you're not going to, and I think the reason is that you're scared. You don't believe I want you for you. But I do."

"It's not that I—"

"But." He cut her off. "I will spend the rest of my life ensuring you're never scared again." And with those words, he pulled a box from his pocket and dropped to one knee.

Liv's heart slammed against her backbone as blood drained from every organ in her body and the sand began to swim in front of her eyes. He was going to propose. Again. "We've already discussed this, Markus," she whispered.

"When I asked you to marry me when you arrived, I asked out of doubt and cynicism." He reached for her hand and then held her cool, limp fingers in his warm and sure grip. "That was wrong."

She began to speak, but he squeezed her hand and she stopped.

"Liv, the love I had for you before has been superseded, trumped, expanded a thousand times, because now I can see who you truly are. All the doubts I had before, all the questions and the disappointment, have been answered in the way I've seen you with those beautiful girls since you arrived here. I should never have carried on taking all those risks when I knew how much it hurt you. You've shown me that, too."

Even though she wanted to clamp her hands over her ears, block out the emotion that was pouring from him, she couldn't deny the effect his words had on her shredded heart. Did he really mean this?

She blinked rapidly. "You're not seeing clearly because you want a family unit for the girls. You're putting all your faith in believing I won't leave you again. Markus, I don't know that I trust *myself* not to run like I always have."

He began stroking his thumb across her trembling fingers. "I'd always believed you were too selfish in love, that you always wanted to put yourself first. Now I've seen how generous you can be, and how you're prepared to put your happiness aside because you love Phoebe and Zoë so deeply. But it doesn't have to be that way."

Liv looked down at the velvet box in his strong fingers, knowing that when he opened it, when he pulled a ring from it as he surely would, she would disappoint him all over again. "But Markus—"

A smile broke across his face as his thumb stroked her fingers. "I'd like to do things properly this time, Liv. On my terms."

He flicked the box open with his thumb, and there was the most beautiful diamond ring Liv had ever seen, winking and dazzling in the morning sunlight.

"I've had this for a while," he said, the smile still tugging at the corner of his mouth. "Quite a few years in fact, and I never thought I'd get the chance to use it. But . . ." He let the box drop and placed the ring at the top of Liv's fourth finger. "Liv, I love you with every part of myself. The part that knows what a wonderful, selfless partner you are. The part that gives thanks for the incredible mother you'll be to Phoebe and Zoë. And the part that wants to give myself to you as lover, friend and husband. Liv, will you do me the greatest honor of marrying me?"

Words crouched paralyzed in her throat. He didn't mean this. He was trusting her too much. And he didn't see how impossible everything had become.

But his eyes. His eyes held more love, more sincerity than she'd ever seen. He'd accepted her completely, and the anguish of having to refuse him, having to deny being part of him, was almost too much to bear.

She dropped to her knees, hoping that by looking him in the eye he'd understand how deeply she meant this, how certain she was that there was no future for them as a real husband and wife. "Oh, Markus. Those words were just too beautiful, and you can't imagine what they mean to me, that you feel I've changed, that you think I'll be a good mother to the girls. But you must know that I can't really marry you. Not in the way you mean."

Instead of looking shocked or pulling back, Markus's face lit with a smile. "You're just scared, Liv. But there's no need to be scared of anything anymore. I'm here to protect you and the girls forever, and you can give in to the feelings for me that I know you have."

She had to make it clear to him, say everything in such a way that he'd know all of the reasons why they couldn't be together. "I'm not scared about you, Markus, I'm realistic about me. I know that I've always run from things and I don't trust that I won't do it again and hurt three people this time."

"You won't, Liv."

"You say that now, but just imagine if I said yes and we got married, *really* married, and something came between us. How do you *know* I wouldn't run? The way I did when I was a kid, when we moved to Paris, when I left you there... I won't put either of us, or the girls, in that position, Markus. Don't you see that by doing this together, by bringing up the girls as friends, we can avoid all that, and we can be honest without emotion, or desire, or even love clouding our expectations as it did in the past?"

A frown began to dig into his forehead, and she wanted to pull him to her, to bury her head in his chest and breathe in the essence of this wonderful, beautiful man that she loved with all of her conflicted heart. But she couldn't. She couldn't comfort him in case she confused everything again, in case her treacherous emotions tangled once more.

They were both quiet for a moment, the hush-hush of the sea the only sound surrounding them. "Will it be too hard to have me around?" She squeezed the words out. "Does me saying no to you mean that you'd rather not do things as we'd planned? Would you rather I take the girls away so that you don't have to be reminded about us every single day?"

"No." His answer was so swift and immediate, like an exclamation point, it indicated there was no doubt in his mind.

The frown remained but Markus didn't let her hand go, the ring still balanced at the end of her finger.

"Do you doubt that I really love you?" he said. "Do you think I'm only saying this so I'll be certain you'll stay here for the girls?"

"No, Markus, of course not. Not now." Her insides crumbled as she realized she was telling the truth. "I've had my doubts about what your true feelings have been but not anymore. And it breaks my heart to think that everything is too late for us."

His face relaxed and he threw her the most bone-melting smile. "I've tried not to love you again, Liv, but I can't. If you tell me no now, I promise I'll never talk like this again, will never push you or compromise anything between us. If you say you won't marry me for love, then I'll accept it. We can look forward now, never back."

Blood pounded in Liv's head as her rational self warred with the sweet, beating desire that was growing—the desire to throw caution to the wind and launch herself into his arms. She dropped her head, and he squeezed her hands once more. He wanted her as her, not just as the mother of the girls he'd fallen in love with.

"You don't have to say it, Liv, I can see the answer in your body."

Tears welled in her eyes and spilled over, but Liv willed every muscle in her body to co-operate so she could lift her head and look this wonderful man squarely in the eye. She wouldn't be a coward any more.

Before she could say anything, he removed the ring from her finger and spoke again. "I'll accept your decision, Liv, but I need you to know that I'll never love anyone but you. You'll be the only mother the girls will ever know, and when you fall in love and marry, you can be sure that I'll still be here to be their dad. Whether you give them brothers or sisters or not, I know you'll be here for them. I know the *real* you now."

Every thought in Liv's head came to a juddering halt.

He was speaking of her falling in love with someone else?

Her having children with another man, but he'd still be here for the girls?

A shiver began at the soles of her feet and worked its way like a tsunami over her skin. He *knew* she'd stay. She could see it in the set of his face and the confidence in his voice.

And he *still* wanted her to be here, even if it meant not being with him.

He stood up and pulled her to her feet. "I respect your reasons for not wanting to be with me, but the power of my love for you will never die. I won't do anything about it because that's what you want, and I won't jeopardize anything for the girls, but I want you to know that I'll always be here for you, and them."

Liv's heart was in free fall and a familiar feeling of vertigo took hold.

He loved her.

Loved her so much that he was going to stay with her and bring up the girls even if she met someone else.

The vertigo spilled over and she searched for a way out.

Leaning into his cotton shirt, she breathed that shaved wood, Markus scent that was far more potent, far more desirable, than anything she'd made in a laboratory, and something kicked deep and hard within her.

She *wanted* this. She wanted him so badly she could taste it. The fact that she was still here, that she hadn't run when it got this tough, germinated a feeling so strong she gasped.

If he believed she'd stay here in spite of what happened between them in the past, if he was prepared to love her from afar but give her her freedom, then the only person stopping them from being together was... her.

She pulled back to look deep in his eyes, and all she saw was unchecked passion and desire. "You love me? You really love me for me? Not just because you're frightened I'll run out on you and the girls?"

The moan of desire that left his mouth answered her

question more than all the words he'd spoken, and she dragged him to her.

"I believe you," she whispered into the rough warmth of his cheek, something cell-deep within her awakening. "I love you, Markus. I love you."

For the first time in her life, someone wanted to put her first—to listen to her, to love her unconditionally and to never leave her—and it caused her heart to crack wide open.

He drew her even closer and brushed his lips across hers, the delicious pain of his stubbled chin causing a moan to leave her throat. With both palms spread across his chest, she kissed him back, hungry to deepen this connection and make this beautiful moment go on forever.

Heat rushed through her body, and for the first time since she'd arrived here, Liv let herself drown in her love for him. She felt safe, whole, and god, loved for herself, and she knew Markus felt the same way.

"I'll love you forever and be by your side always, Liv." They were the words she'd imagined over and over since she'd been here, but nothing could have prepared her for the way they floated through the air and landed straight inside her heart.

"I was scared," she managed to say through trembling lips. "That I'd run again when it all got too tough. I tried to push my love for you away, but I can't. I love you, Markus. I've always loved you. But I'm not scared anymore. Seeing you with the girls, loving them and protecting them, makes me know you'll do that for me too."

She kissed him again—on his cheeks, his eyelids, his mouth—before she drew back gasping. "I want to be your wife because I love you with all my heart and because you've given me the greatest gifts I could have hoped for—a family

I belong in, a place to be safe, and a love that makes my heart sing—"

She wanted to say more, and she would, every day she was Markus's wife, but for now her words were sweetly smothered by his kiss.

EPILOGUE

"Ｙou go for your walk, dear." Markus's mom, Mila, smiled at Liv as they cleared the outside dinner table. Dusk had settled and the toasty scent of dry summer grass blew in on a gentle breeze.

"And when you get back we'll check out the old home movies I brought over with us," said Markus's brother, Alex, through the open kitchen window. "I have indisputable proof that your husband once rocked a mullet and that he's always had a shocking sense of style."

"Hey, there are some pretty choice shots of you geeking out with your stamp collection and your dalliance with over-sized jeans," his wife Mara said as she playfully swiped at him.

"I can't wait! Thanks, Mom," Liv said, shooting her mother-in-law a grin. "It's so hot a quick dip might be a good idea. This little turbo heater doesn't stop." She stroked the firm bump under her sundress.

"I've got towels." Markus came through the French doors onto the deck then hugged her from behind, spreading both hands over her swelling tummy. "Thanks Mom, it's so great to have you guys here. Makes me realize how much I miss Dad's cooking."

"You all bring us so much joy," his mother said, her eyes sparkling. You and your brother have chosen such incredible women as your wives. We are all so lucky."

Liv's heart squeezed as Markus kissed his mother on the cheek.

"Don't let those two little monkeys keep you up," he said. "Dad's still in there reading them stories, and they've got Petro sitting in the rocking chair untangling their kite strings."

"Would you look at that," Markus's mom murmured as she looked out across the bay, and they all turned toward the moon that was rising over the pewter sea. "What a fabulous evening."

The ripe, round orb sat above the bay as Markus led Liv by the hand down to the water. Sweet perfume from the lavender bushes wafted around them as they walked the familiar path to the beach. "I think this is the first full moon we've had since we've been back from Brentwood Bay." He chuckled. "The first that we've had at Aphrodite's Rock since we've been married."

"Oh, you're right," Liv said as they reached the beach and her toes luxuriated in the cool touch of sand and pebbles. "I guess your Mom and Dad know all about the legend. They'll be here three months of the year and sharing this place with their friendly neighborhood goddess."

"Do you think we might catch them stealing away for a quick swim?" Markus grinned.

"By the way your dad looks at your mom, I don't think they need too much of Aphrodite's help. Do you think we'll be like that when we're their age?" Liv asked as she squeezed his hand. "Or like Ana-Maria and Petro, secretly holding hands when they think no one's looking?"

Markus stopped at the water's edge and drew her to him before nuzzling at her neck. "Are you kidding? We'll still be like that when we've got great-grandchildren. We'll have to build ten new wings on the house to accommodate everyone."

"Hey," Liv said, pushing him back and smiling. "It's a full moon. You know what that means. Maybe we can swim around the rock tonight."

She'd never done it. Never tested the theory that Aphrodite would give her true love if she swam three times around the rock naked. She hadn't needed to perform some ritual to know that she was with the love of her life. It was clear every day—in the way her body melted when he touched her, the way her heart burst when he read stories to Phoebe and Zoë, and the way he looked at her when he stroked her growing belly. But it would be fun to say they'd done it.

"Come on," she said, excitement bubbling within her as she peeled off her T-shirt to reveal her rounded belly. "Let's see if the legend's true. Let's see if it works."

But before she could dip her toes into the surf, Markus stopped her and turned her toward him. "No, Liv."

His loving gaze held her still, and his warm palms smoothed her forearms.

What did he mean? Didn't he believe the legend?

"Come on, baby." She laughed as she tickled his chest. "I want everlasting love. I want to swim around that rock so that I know you'll be the one for me forever."

He drew her to him until his lips grazed her ear, and she trembled at the rich, deep tone of his words. "There's no need for us to do it."

"Why not?" She looked up into his beautiful face, confused. He didn't believe the legend anymore? Didn't want to test the theory in case it didn't come true?

"Because, my darling, I've already done it."

She gasped. "When?"

"When I came here from Paris without you. When I was lost and lonely and wishing I had you in my arms. It seemed like the only thing I could do to keep alive the possibility that you'd come back to me one day."

He leaned down and kissed her fully on the mouth, before she placed both palms on his chest and looked into his eyes.

Her voice was a whisper. "You mean you came down here, stripped off and swam three times around the rock?"

"And thought of the one woman I wanted to be with always. My true and everlasting love."

"So, it works then," she whispered as she leaned in to kiss him. "It works."

***

Thank you so much for reading *A Family for Good*. I hope you love Liv, Markus and the girls as much as I do.

Find out what else is happening in Brentwood Bay in the *Breaking Through* series! You can find Book I *Bad Reputations* as an e book on Amazon, or ask for it at your local book store or library. You can read the prologue and Chapter One of *Bad Reputations* on the next page.

And to find out about new releases, sign up for my newsletter **here or email** barb@barbaradeleo.com. When you sign up I'll send you the **FREE** prequel to the Tall, Dark and Driven series, ***Waiting on Forever - Alex's story***!

I hugely appreciate your help in spreading the word about my books, including telling a friend. Reviews help readers find books! Please review *A Family for Good* **here** or on your favorite site.

THE BREAKING THROUGH SERIES
PROLOGUE

*a*nd now I'd like you to take a moment to centre yourself, look deep within your most secret places to determine the barriers that you're unconsciously putting in your way to success in life."

Bah....loney!

Kirin Hart yanked out the ear pods that still carried the softly irritating voice of Sapphire Green - *Whole Life Coach* - and skated them across her desk. Surely she wasn't the only one in this online coaching session to have aching molars every time Sapphire asked them to "dig beneath your fragile facade" and "stop stroking your immature ego."

Kirin blew away her bangs with a hot breath and leaned back in her chair. She scanned the names of the twenty-four other people on this call. Were they women? Men? Business people? Students?

Sapphire had insisted everyone would be completely anonymous, so people had some wildly made-up names. There was "BlueWolverine" who was trying to learn how to be assertive with their mother-in-law; "Lucy Lu" who was trying to decide if they should change careers; and Kirin's favorite "Bottomless Brenda" who was having some complex family issues she wanted to address once and for all.

Kirin clicked on the icon next to Brenda's name and a separate chat window popped up.

Kirin: *How's your flimsy facade looking, Brenda?*
Bottomless Brenda: 😊 Three dots that indicated Brenda was still writing.
Bottomless Brenda: *My immature ego's gone off sulking in the corner to eat Ben and Jerry's Salted Caramel. If yours wants to play hooky maybe we can hang for a while.*
Kirin: 🍸 *Here voluntarily or dragged kicking and screaming?*
Bottomless Brenda: *Kinda voluntarily. As I said in my intro I've got some family stuff going on and wanted to get a handle on how to tackle it. Didn't want to be doing that face-to-face in a small town.*
Kirin: *Your real name Bottomless Brenda?*
Bottomless Brenda: 😊 *No, and believe me I've got plenty of bottom.* 😄 *I make store mannequins, so I'm often surrounded by headless torsos. Men from the waist up. My name's Gwin.*

Men from the waist up. Wouldn't that solve a whole lot of my problems, Kirin thought.

Kirin: 🍸 *Cool name, Gwin. Short for something?*
Gwin: *Guinevere, as in King Arthur and stuff.* 😊 *My mom's Avalon too so it's all my Nan's fault. What brings you to Sapphire's den. Are you here because of your name?*

Kirin's eyes darted to the name she'd given herself. Surely Gwin hadn't worked out who she was? She'd been super

careful not to reference her job or anything that might iden-
tify her. "Broken Hearted." *Broken Hart*. That just about
summed her up.

Kirin: *Not at all. Just a silly play on words.* 😄 *It's more the way
I feel every Tuesday at 8pm when we have to go online* 🙄
Gwin: *Kiwi6 is a bit of a laugh. That story she told the first day
about being traumatised by a rabbit made of jello made me wet
my pants.*
Kirin: 🤣 *Let's ask if she wants to play hooky, too*
Gwin: 👋

Kirin clicked on *Add to Chat* and typed in *Kiwi6*. "Want to
hang out?" she typed. "Promise it's a jello rabbit free zone."

Kiwi6: *Hey Brenda and Broken Hearted. Nice to meet you. I was
trying to dig deep but couldn't get past the custard donut I had
about half an hour ago* 🍩
Kirin: 😄 *Just call me, Kay. And this is Gwin.*
Gwin: *I'm guessing you're from New Zealand, Kiwi?* 🥝
Kiwi6: *I'm Ellie and yes I'm in New Zealand right now. You
guys?*
Gwin: *I'm in Brentwood Bay, Northern California. Born, raised
and still here unfortunately* 🌁 *You, Kay?*

"San Francisco," Kirin typed, enjoying the fact she could
be anonymous. Someone from New Zealand wouldn't know
who she was, but someone from California could.

Gwin: *I guess that's the beauty of the online world. We can all be
anyone from anywhere. Kinda levels the playing field.*

Doesn't it just, Kirin thought.

Ellie: *It's kinda not what I imagined, this course. I thought we'd get more practical ways to organize our lives, set goals, that sort of thing. I spend the hour feeling pretty 💩 about myself and then spend the next seven days worrying that I haven't done all the homework she's set.*

Gwin: Oh, I HEAR you!

Kirin: *What made you take the course?*

Ellie: *I'm back home in New Zealand to do a community project and it's kinda delicate so I wanted to give myself a few assertiveness skills.*

Kirin: *I've always wanted to go to New Zealand.*

Ellie: *I've spent most of the last few years in the States which is where I heard about Sapphire. It's lovely to be home.*

Gwin: *A community project sounds fun. What sort?*

Ellie: *It's quite a big thing. I need to get the whole town on board so I was hoping this might give me some inspiration for how to stay strong.*

Gwin: *Thinking you'll have some resistance?*

Ellie: *Yes resistance, and some ghosts that I'm going to have to revisit .*

Kirin: *Kinda like a high school reunion. When you know you really shouldn't care about what everyone will think of you but some deep, sick part of yourself is desperate for them to see you as accomplished and cool now.*

Ellie: *Exactly. And you Kay? Why did you sign?*

Kirin: *I didn't want to. It's a condition of my probation.*

There was a distinct pause in messaging.

Kirin: 🙄🙄🙄 *Oh, not THAT kind of probation!!!!* 🏆

I've been told by my board I need an image makeover. I'm on a kind of behaviour probation. . .

Gwin: *What the ACTUAL! Please don't tell me it's a guy who's told you that!!* 🫣

Kirin: *It's a few guys and a couple of women. They're on my company board and apparently my image is bringing down the brand so they want to give me a zjuszh up – (don't know if that's the way you spell it!)*

Ellie: *Your image as in the way you look? Clearly I can't see you, but I can already tell you're friendly and quick and you're funny. Who cares what you look like?*

Kirin: *Everyone in the business except me apparently. How about you Gwin? Think this course is going to help you with your family stuff?*

Gwin:. 🫥 *I don't know anymore. I'm trying to get my sister and niece to move out of my mom's house and move to the city. Things are a bit wobbly for my niece - she's fourteen - and I'd kinda like to see her have different teenage years to me and her mom.*

Ellie: *And your mom doesn't want you to go?*

Gwin: *You've got it. I'm twenty-nine. I don't think it's too unreasonable for me not to want my mom folding my underwear anymore* 🫠 *.*

Kirin: *Will your mom have a good support network after you leave?*

Gwin: *She knows the whole town. She's had a hairdressing salon since she was in her twenties and she's got a tight group of girlfriends. We've told her to come to the city with us but she won't even consider it* 🫤 *.*

Kirin: *You know I have got one useful thing from this whole course....When she asked us what we're afraid of...*

Ellie: *Yeah, I agree, that was quite helpful. Want to share?*

Kirin: *I guess I'm afraid that if people see that my outside doesn't match my inside they won't believe in me anymore.*

Gwin: *I still don't really understand why you need to change your image so much. How do you think those people see you now?*

Kirin: *That I'm too old fashioned, that I only appeal to a small group of people. They think if they modernise me, I'll expand the brand.*

Ellie: *Any part of you think they could be right?*

Kirin: *Yeah, I get what they mean but I resent the fact that my skills can't speak for themselves. How about you guys? Did you do the fear exercise* 😮*?*

Gwin: *Yeah, it was pretty easy for me. I'm afraid of my niece having a challenging life like my sister's had. Getting into the same sorts of risky situations. Also not having the same little life her mom and I have both had.*

Kirin: *Little life?*

Gwin: *When people know you – or they think you do. They know your family, your history, that time you had a meltdown in the faucet aisle at Home Depot. Sometimes that's a great thing, but often it can just lead to a whole lot of judgment.*

Ellie: *I just realized, you're about to do the opposite of me. You're breaking away from the life that's defined you for so long and I'm breaking back in.*

Gwin: *And what part of that makes you afraid?*

Ellie: *Having to revisit some tough things that happened to me back there. Face memories that hurt a lot* 😔*.*

Kirin: *That's a whole lot of pressure to have to face up to. How long will you have to be there?*

Ellie: *A few months. I've done a lot of ground work and now I'm here I'll need to call some town meetings and get the project started. Things could get spiky.*

Gwin: *Anyone special with you for support* 🖤*?*

Ellie: *No. I've been too busy organising everything to be dating lately. You guys?*

Kirin: *HELL. NO. I was separated and almost divorced when my husband died a few years ago. and I'm completely off dating for the next millennium or so. How about you Gwin? Leaving anyone behind in Brentwood Bay.*

Gwin: *No. I live with my Mom, my sister and my niece so dating hasn't been easy. My sister will leave a string of broken hearts. Who knows what might happen for me in the big city though?*

Kirin: *You know what, you guys? I've got more out of this chat than I have from every Tuesday put together. Why don't we keep this up?*

Elie: *You mean chat on a Tuesday instead of listen to Sapphire?*

Kirin: *Yes! Like we're a lifeboat of three, helping each other navigate the next few months together.*

Gwin: *BEST IDEA! I've got amazing girlfriends and really good work mates, but in a small town it's sometimes hard to be completely honest about what you're feeling, you know I'd love to be able to share that stuff with you guys* 💚.

Ellie: *I can understand that. Not wanting anything to get back to your family. LOVE this idea, Kay. My sister will be here for a bit while I'm working on the project, but she went through the same tough time I did when I was last here and we've kind of never talked about the really hard stuff, you know.*

Kirin: *Hugs for that* 🫂. *Okay, why don't we say the one big thing we want to achieve this week and then we can cheer lead each other on when we meet back next Tuesday.*

Gwin: *Okay. I want to convince my sister that us leaving town* 🕊️ *is the best thing for the three of us and for us to start putting plans in place. You, Ellie?*

Ellie: *To have the strength to go back to Rata Cove and have some quiet time there by myself before I have to call town meetings.* 🐢 *What about you Kay?*

Kirin: *I want to bite my tongue, see the bigger picture and the greater good for the business. Maybe try not to have the next image consultant quit.* 😊
Okay, girls, It's a date!!

You can read the synopsis and first chapter of Book One in the **Breaking Through** series—**Bad Reputations–Kirin's story** on the next pages.

BAD REPUTATIONS
KIRIN'S STORY

Image consultant Blake Matthews is facing his toughest PR challenge yet: salvage the reputation of celebrity chef Kirin Hart. Once he does, he'll be able to acquire San Francisco's most successful PR firm. But Kirin's no easy fix. She's stubborn about changing her comfortable homemaker image and is unapologetic for wanting to present her authentic self after her ex-husband trashed their collective public image. She needs a PR lifeline fast. Only problem is that Blake wants more than to make her over . . .

Kirin doesn't believe she needs a makeover—her true fans love will love her as she is. But she could lose everything if the scandal perpetuated by her ex, and the loss of reputation that has followed it, doesn't get quashed right away. Kirin agrees to let model-perfect Blake work his magic for two weeks, but things get complicated when she can't deny the way her body flares to life when he's near.

You can read an extract from *Bad Reputations* over the page.

BAD REPUTATIONS - CHAPTER ONE

BOOK ONE

Chapter One

Blake Matthews stepped from the elevator into the cool basement of Hart Corporation and sucked in a lungful of air. The sweet smell of something toasted and warm assaulted his nose, filled his mouth, and confirmed that Kirin Hart, America's fallen-angel chef, was close by.

Hands slung in his pockets, he strode down the bare concrete corridor toward the enticing smells and cooking sounds, ready to meet the challenge of fixing Mrs. Hart's public image that had been so spectacularly annihilated.

Because she'd broken the last consultant who'd tried to tackle this mammoth assignment, he'd stepped in to minimize catastrophic fallout to the PR company he was about to buy. The board of directors had given him fourteen days to prove he had what it took to preserve the integrity of their company or they wouldn't sell to him.

He'd turn the situation around in ten.

A photograph from the file his investigator had put together reeled through his mind—the focused woman carefully disguised beneath homely outfits, pastel cardigans, and blond hair in a sweet plait. She'd certainly crafted the look of dependable domestic goddess well. Pity her husband and the other half of *Cooking with Hart* had died mid coitus with a much younger woman, thereby smashing their wholesome image and the public's love for them to smithereens. If that wasn't bad enough, a male staffer ten years her junior then accused her of sexual harassment and now her business was in free fall.

Confidence pumped sweetly through his veins. He'd never failed at a job this big, and didn't intend to start now, especially with the expansion of his business at stake. He'd overhaul Mrs. Hart—beige trouser suit and all—and be back home in New York in no time.

At the end of the corridor, he stopped in an open doorway.

Behind a long stainless-steel counter strewn with cooking paraphernalia, a woman had her back to him as she stirred something on an enormous industrial stove. He leaned a shoulder against the doorjamb, the low roar of overhead fans sucking away steam allowing him to watch her unnoticed. He made the most of the sight.

A loose blond ponytail, falling from beneath a small black hat, rested between narrow shoulders. His gaze tracked lower to where the strings of a black chef's apron fell down the back of a plain tan skirt hugging a perfectly rounded bottom. He took a step into the room but still she worked, backward and forward. Her movements were sexily hypnotic—stirring and shuffling implements, occasionally dusting a hand across the curve of her hip—oblivious to the fact he couldn't pull his eyes away.

Still unaware of him, she leaned to the back of the stove, dipped a spoon into one of the pans, and steadying a hand beneath, lifted it to her face and blew. As she opened her mouth and slowly slid the spoon between dusky lips, the secret intimacy of it caused his stomach muscles to clench, and on reflex he cleared his throat. When she spun around, the spoon clattered to the floor, her glistening mouth forming a perfect O.

"Can I help you?" She reached for a cloth to clean up the liquid splattered across the counter and all down her front. "You must be lost."

He stepped into the room. "Not lost. I was looking for you. Don't stop what you're doing, I was enjoying it." He moved forward. "Blake—"

"How did you get in? This is a restricted area." Her eyes flicked to her apron and back at him, the creamy skin at her jaw tightening as she wiped away the mess.

"Through the door." He tried a grin, but she dropped her gaze.

"But I have security."

The chilly reception wasn't surprising. Angela Jenkins, the original consultant on this job, had described Kirin Hart as defensive and suspicious—and that was before Kirin had told her that she didn't need their services any more. "Might want to check on that security." He stepped around a stack of cardboard cartons. "I told your doorman who I was, and he let me come straight down."

Finally, sparking caramel eyes focused on him and she stilled. "What can I do for you?"

He pulled up an industrial looking stool and sat. "If you're not going to continue cooking, best turn the stoves off. This could take a while."

She laid both hands on the counter and hooked him with a "give me orders if you dare" look as her chest rose then fell. "The expansion might've fallen through, but I still need these new stoves." The mask was edged with hard-nosed determination and was even more of a turn on than watching her cook. Her tongue peeped out and she moistened her lips. "I'll downsize the chillers, though, so you can take the large one in the next room. It was the last you sent."

She began to remove the apron and her body was revealed. A cream blouse in soft fabric skimmed her breasts and sat lightly across a gently rounded stomach. It had a V-neck but must have had two dozen tiny pearl buttons all down the front and reminded him of a particularly up-tight Sunday school teacher he'd once had.

At her throat, a thin gold chain lay against her milky skin with the letter K in a flourishing script. "We won't be needing the new office furniture you delivered last month either. You can take that back." She waved a delicate hand and thin gold bracelets tinkled on her wrist. "I'm sorry but I don't have time to discuss this right now." She turned back to the stove. "Make an appointment with my P.A. and she'll coordinate with you. I'm sure you'll find your way out."

He raised an eyebrow, intrigued by her ball-breaking attitude and the fact they'd had an entire conversation without him saying a word.

If he was a supplier of cooking equipment, or a repo man, he'd be throwing out some pretty choice expletives right now in response to an attitude like that. Lucky for her, he had a few more manners than she was displaying. No wonder she was such a PR disaster. He shrugged out of his suit jacket and finding nowhere to put it on the crowded counter, laid it across his knee. "I've come to discuss your contract with Dent and Douglas."

Her shoulders straightened. "My contract with Dent and Douglas is finished. I explained to Angela Jenkins that it wasn't working out." She turned and began to play with the strings of the apron. "If there are things to sign my lawyer will take care of it."

She leaned closer and the K slipped beneath the fabric to a part of her he couldn't see.

He swallowed then refocused. Given her significant business troubles, the fight she still had left inside was admirable, and surprisingly sexy. "I'm Angela's replacement."

Her cinnamon eyes darted from the apron to his face. "May I see your card?"

Shit. His stomach clenched. He was going to have enough trouble making her come around if she thought he worked for Dent and Douglas. If she knew he was D and D's new buyer and that they wouldn't sell until he'd fixed her, she'd be the one in the driver's seat, and no way was that happening. His real identity could be saved for later. "I left my last card with your guy upstairs. Call him."

She turned as if looking for her phone then seemed to think better of it. "In case you haven't quite gotten the message, I've changed my mind. I don't want an image consultant anymore. Thanks for your time I'm sorry it was wasted."

Good. She believed him. But he wasn't going anywhere. "No consultant? Why?"

There was that tongue again, slipping between her lips, and he found his eyes being constantly pulled there. "Because I need to get *myself* out of this mess." A flare of pain blossomed in her eyes.

So, there was a heart beating behind that tough shell. "And how do you intend to do that on your own? From what I understand, your brand's looking about as attractive as a high-speed train wreck right now. And you're the one who's still standing on the accelerator. Seems to me like you need a lot of professional help. Fast."

She pulled the hat from her head and tiny blond hairs stood up at different angles. The pain was still in her eyes and her face had softened. "By working hard, cooking well, things I've done since the start of my career. No amount of PR speak and fancy outfits is going to do that for me."

He picked up some sort of metal cooking utensil and turned the handle. "I'd suggest it wasn't your cooking or your work ethic that got you into this mess so it's not likely they'll get you out. Your brother did the right thing hiring the best PR firm in town to turn your fortunes around. You'll never put this right on your own. From what I understand, if you don't act soon you're going to have a parade of removal companies banging down your door. And they might not be as gentlemanly as me."

She'd rolled the apron into a ball and threw it to the side. "Flynn has a good heart, but he has no clue about this industry." She rubbed her forehead. "Your colleague, Angela, started telling me what I should wear, how I should speak, who I should be associating with." Her eyes flashed as she spoke.

"All good advice which I hear you refused to take."

She laid a hand at her throat, her slim fingers stroking the pale skin that looked as silky as the fabric covering the rest of her top half. "What did you say your name was?"

"Matthews." He threw her his 'trust-me' smile. "Blake Matthews."

"Well, thanks, Blake Matthews but I don't require the services of Dent and Douglas anymore. I'm happy to handle this on my own." She picked up a towel and turned back toward the stove. "If you don't mind, I have a party to cater." She knelt, looked in an oven then pulled open the door.

"What's the party?"

She leaned in and put a skewer into the cake. When she drew it back he noticed her long, dark lashes as she surveyed the end. "It's for the daughter of a friend."

"Sweet Sixteen? Or twenty-first? You must be glad for the work. I've heard that the catering side of Hart Corp. has taken a big hit." He turned the handle on the cooking thing and a blade inside nearly sliced his finger off.

She shut the oven door and turned, skewer pointing toward him, cheeks flushed. "It's Maura's fourth birthday, and unless you want to lose a thumb, I suggest you put that down. There's a reason we don't let the public down here."

The public? Prickles rose on his neck for a second and then he reminded himself how much he enjoyed the challenge of getting people like Kirin Hart on his side. Two could play at her game.

He nodded slowly and placed the cutting thing gently on the counter. "How long have you been catering birthday parties for pre-schoolers? And is that sort of work going to stop your business imploding? Can't imagine there's a whole lot of profit in Jell-O molds and Funnell cakes, or whatever kids eat at parties these days."

She sighed. "My business is none of *your* business, Mr. Matthews."

"Ah, but that's where you're wrong." He met the challenging spark in her stare and smiled slowly. He'd come from New York to buy Dent and Douglas—the jewel in his crown of image consultancies and PR firms—and suddenly they'd put a halt to the sale. The Hart Corp debacle—and the resulting media circus—was destroying the reputation San Francisco's most famous PR company had worked fifty years to develop. They wanted proof that Blake had the capacity to maintain the integrity of their name. And they wouldn't sell until he'd proven he could fix Kirin Hart and her image.

He put his palms flat on the cool counter top. "I don't do failure, Ms. Hart, and right now Dent and Douglas has a contracted client whose image hasn't been changed, whose fortunes haven't been turned around as they assured her they would be. Where I come from, we call that a dud rap. I don't do dud raps. In fact, I've never been involved in one, and don't intend to start now."

Kirin tucked a stray piece of hair behind her ear. "Angela spent her whole time suggesting I didn't know how to dress or do my hair. I'm a chef not a catwalk model, Mr. Matthews. Surely the decision about whether to carry on a contract is up to the client," she said, voice tight.

"That might be the case if that client wasn't the biggest image disaster in American history. The whole world and his PR machine know D and D took you on. Their reputation will be worth nothing if we don't see the contract through."

She took a moment before answering. "And why are you so interested in me? Are you the bad cop, the guy who tries to muscle in and rough up the client when she's not toeing the line?"

He adjusted himself on the stool, hooked by her candor and the way her chest rose in defiance. He hadn't counted on her spitfire responses, or his responses to them. He'd dealt with a lot of people in his career, but no one had captured his fascination as quickly as Kirin Hart. This was a woman who believed in herself and her image so much she was prepared to fight to the death for it. Trouble was, the media was nailing the lid on her career's coffin hour-by-hour and unless something drastic happened, she'd have nothing left. And his plan to add the crowning company in his coast-to-coast empire would be finished.

"I'm no bad cop, and I'm not interested in you, Ms. Hart, I'm interested in your image. They're two entirely different things. When you begin to understand that, we might start getting somewhere."

For a second something passed across her face, almost as if she'd been hurt by what he'd said but then she stood straighter. "I've told you, I'm not interested. I'll pay the contract break fee and be done with it. And please don't call me Ms. Hart, my name is Kirin."

"You'll renege on the contract and just wait for everything to go up in a smoke of debts? All the things you've worked so hard and so long for?"

The skewer clanged as she dropped it on the counter top. "People have been taking from me since my husband died, Mr. Matthews." Her lip trembled before she cleared her throat. "In fact, since well before that and right up to the present day. I'm used to it, but I'm not going to let you do it, too."

"You mean your husband's affair? The fact he died when he was with his mistress? Or the sexual harassment accusation against you."

Blood drained from her face and her eyes glistened. "You know about all of it?"

He crossed his arms. "The way I understand it, firstly your husband single handedly smashed your career, your livelihood and image, and then a low life decided to kick you while you were down. You want that false accusation to be the way you're remembered? And for everything you worked for before your husband's deception to be worth nothing?"

"It's already happened," she murmured and looked up at

him. Her shoulders had slumped and the defeated look on her face stirred something deep inside. For the shortest second, her cultivated control was replaced with soft vulnerability, and the contrast was mesmerizing. She lifted her chin and whispered, "No. No, I don't want to be remembered that way."

"Then let me help you."

She picked up a knife and sliced it through a piece of butter. "I've been relying on people for too long. It's time I took charge."

He swallowed, his heart throwing in an extra beat for her vulnerability. "I'm the best there is at turning around public images, Kirin. Come back on board and I'll have journalists phoning you for interviews, invitations to talk shows and A-list parties. I can have your image back on track, brighter than you ever thought possible, in no time."

She reached behind her for a small copper pot and put the butter in. "And what makes you so sure you can achieve this magic? Is a superhero outfit lurking under that smart suit?" Her first real smile flitted across her face and it dazzled. "A pair of underpants over the tights beneath? I don't need rescuing by you or anyone else, Mr. Matthews."

He didn't usually have to spell out his experience. Most people he dealt with had been on a waiting list for his services for months and knew every last detail. "I've been in the image industry for fourteen years. I started work at sixteen as an international model and quickly learned that the way you portray yourself can make, or cost you, millions. The image the public currently has of you, if I may be so blunt, is a woman who is down trodden and beaten. I can already tell that's not the real you at all."

She was quiet for a moment then shook her head. "Thanks for your interest but I'm going to do this on my own. Now, if you don't mind, I have a hundred cupcakes to frost."

Blake reached into his pocket, pulled out his phone and swiped to the picture he wanted before sliding it across the counter to her. "How's this 'doing it on your own' working out for you?"

She looked down at the picture on the screen and a flush swept up her neck. "Not one of my finest moments."

"You flipped the bird at twenty-five photographers and the image spread across nationwide news channels and is now viral on Tik Tok. If this is part of your strategy to go it alone, can I quietly suggest you're making a dog's breakfast of it? My research tells me you've been hounded by photographers for weeks, that you even had to have one removed from your front yard, all reasons to be upset, but the middle finger salute doesn't quite fit with your current image."

The tongue came out and swept across her lip again and in an unbidden flash, his pulse spiked. He suffocated the rogue reaction and focused.

"How much do you know about cooking, Mr. Matthews, and how much about my career?"

"It's Blake," he said. "I know that you and your husband started young and built a multi-million dollar business. People saw your shows, your cookbooks, your grocery products, the whole, 'Cooking with Hart' brand as defining integrity, reflecting traditional values and wholesome living. I also know that your husband cheated on you with a much younger woman and made a lie of the down home and dependable brand you'd both so carefully created."

Kirin had switched off the stoves and fans and leaned against the counter. A connection was growing. "And the rest of it?"

"I know that some said your husband wandered because

you were too ruthless and controlling, too hard and business like. Sexist and ignorant clearly, but perception is everything."

Her eyes rounded and she stood motionless. "And do you believe that's really what I'm like?"

He shrugged and pinned his gaze to hers. "What I believe is irrelevant. What the public currently sees is a woman who's still trying to present an image of traditional values and buttoned down control. A woman who has become an enigma— someone they don't really know anymore and it's taken the focus right away from what you're best at—your cooking business. Not only will all that go away if you agree to my plan, but we can harness that new image of you to build a whole new brand."

"And what would your strategy be? To tell me to change the way I dress, the way I speak, like Angela did?"

"There would be some of that," he admitted. "And a few lessons in what *not* to say."

She reached across to a pile of linen and pulled out a fresh apron and hat. "Thank you for your time, Mr. Matthews. I appreciate your interest and concern, but part of what's wrong in my life is that I've put too much of my trust in people—especially pushy men—who've only wanted to use me for their own gains. You're not going to be another of those people, so I thank you for your time. Please close the door behind you." And with that, she turned her back and walked away.

You can buy **Bad Reputations** on Amazon here or ask for it at your local book store or library.

FANCY A FREE NOVELLA?

Throughout my career, my readers have been such a key part of my writing life, and I love to keep them up to date with what I'm doing. I occasionally send out newsletters with details on new releases and extra special offers for both my books and others like mine. I promise I won't bombard you!

If you sign up to the mailing list, the first thing I'll send you is a **FREE** novella, *Waiting on Forever*, is Alex and Mara's story, and the prequel to my *Tall, Dark and Driven* series.

Waiting on Forever

One last task to complete, then Alex Panos can fulfill a heart-breaking promise. That is, if he can get past cute and quirky Mara Hemmingway.

On her own since she was sixteen, Mara won't be taken advantage of again—especially not by brooding and troubled Alex. Instead, she'll play him at his own game.

When their powerful attraction threatens to get in the way of both their dreams, someone will have to face a future of waiting on forever.

You can get the novella by signing up here or emailing barb@barbaradeleo.com.

APPLY TO JOIN BARBARA'S REVIEW TEAM!

If you really enjoyed *A Family for Good* and fancy reading a lot more about the crazy, lovable people of Brentwood Bay, apply to join Barbara's review team!

Barbara is now taking applications to join her Advanced Review team. If you're selected, you'll get all of Barbara's releases free, up to a month before release!

Fill out an application **here** or email: barb@barbaradeleo.com

ABOUT BARBARA

Multi award winning author, Barbara DeLeo's first book, co-written with her best friend, was a story about beauty queens in space. She was eleven, and the sole, handwritten copy was lost years ago much to everyone's relief. It's some small miracle that she kept the faith and now lives her dream of writing sparkling contemporary romance with unforgettable characters.

Degrees in English and Psychology, and a career as an English teacher, fueled Barbara's passion for people and stories, and a number of years living in Europe —primarily in Athens, Greece—gave her a love for romantic settings.

Discovering she was having her second set of twins in two years, Barbara knew she must be paying penance for being disorganized in a previous life and now uses every spare second to create her stories.With every word she writes, Barbara is sharing her belief in the transformational power of loving relationships.

Married to her winemaker hero for twenty two years, Barbara's happiest when she's getting to know her latest cast of characters. She still loves telling stories about finding love in all the wrong places, but now without a beauty queen or spaceship in sight.

facebook.com/BarbaraDeleoAuthor
twitter.com/BarbDeLeo

A Family for Good
A Tall, Dark and Driven book
Markus's story
by Barbara DeLeo

This book is a work of fiction. Names, characters, places and incidents are the product of the author's imagination or are used fictitiously. Any resemblance to actual events, locales, or persons, living or dead, is coincidental.

Cover Design - Natasha Snow Designs www.natashasnow.com

ALSO BY BARBARA DELEO

The Tall, Dark and Driven series

All books can be read as stand alone

Waiting on Forever—prequel novella ~ **Alex's story** ~ available **FREE** here or email barb@barbaradeleo.com

Ask for Barbara DeLeo's books at your local bookstore, library, or on the Amazon links below.

Making the Love List —**Book 1~Yasmin's story** ~ available on Amazon here .

Winning the Wedding War—**Book 2~Nick's story** ~ available on Amazon here.

Reining in the Rebel —**Book 3 ~Ari's story**~ available on Amazon here.

A Home for Summer—**Book 4 ~ Costa's story** ~ available on Amazon here.

A Marriage for Show—**Book 5 ~ Christo's story** ~ available on Amazon here.

———————

The Breaking Through series

All books can be read as stand alone.

Bad Reputations—Book 1 ~ Kirin's story

available here.

ACKNOWLEDGEMENTS

*N*ot only was I lucky enough to have been born into a wonderfully supportive family where dreams are championed and crazy little quirks celebrated, I've been welcomed into a second family too. Since I met my Greek boyfriend, now husband, thirty years ago, I've been immersed in a culture, a language, and a way of celebrating life that I love. I'd like to thank both families for giving me love, laughter, and inspiration for the story of the Katsalos family in my *Tall, Dark and Driven* series.

My heartfelt thanks also goes to:

My agent, Nalini Akolekar, who always has my back and wonderful advice to share.

My incredible crit partners: Hayson Manning and Rachel Bailey, who are amazing writers and save my patootie time and time again.

Iona, Sue, Kate, Courtney, Deborah, Nadine and Naomi who are the BEST group of motivators, cheerleaders and wine drinking pals a girl could have.

My cover designer: Natasha Snow, who nails it every time.

My copy editor: Elizabeth King from Type A Editing Her attention to detail is legendary.

My proofreader: Amy Hart who makes everything shine.

My cheer squad: Lyn, Lee, Barb, Ann, Asra, Quinn, Jolene, Manisha, Elsie, MacKenzie, Marni, Mae, Jody and Amber.

And to George and my four amazing children, thank you for helping me to keep on living this dream. Squeeze, squeeze, squeeze.

Barb X

Manufactured by Amazon.ca
Bolton, ON